They were lost.

"Great, now I'm cold and my clothes are soaked," Lena complained.

Colt ground his hips against her, making a ribbon of need wind slowly through her body.

"I'm sure we can find a way to keep you warm."

"Oh, yeah." She arched her back and pressed her breasts against the expanse of his chest.

She wanted to touch him, taste him.... And here was as good a place as any.

Reaching between them, she wiggled her hand down under the edge of his waistband.

"I was talking about building a fire," Colt said, a grin playing at the corners of his mouth.

"Jerk," she grumbled, suppressing her own smile.

She took a step away, but Colt pulled her back into his arms, stealing her breath with a kiss.

Maybe being lost wasn't so bad after all....

Dear Reader,

I began brainstorming my Island Nights series in the middle of one of the coldest winters we've had in a long time. Let me tell you, slipping away to a romantic tropical island sure seemed like a wonderful idea! Writing these books allowed me that opportunity in my mind if not in real life.

I started wondering what kinds of people might visit a remote tropical resort. Honeymooners were an obvious choice, especially as I started fleshing out Escape's unique history and business model. We're talking about Blaze here, so of course Escape caters to adults looking for a bit of fantasy. But what if the fantasy fell apart, the wedding didn't happen and the bride ended up on the island with her very hot—and very male—best friend....

Add a local legend about finding your heart's desire—whether it's what you were looking for or not—and you've got the recipe for some sexy, sultry beachside fun.

I had such a good time writing Lena and Colt's story, and I hope you enjoy it as much as I did! I'd love to hear what you think. You can contact me at Kira@KiraSinclair.com or visit my website, www.KiraSinclair.com.

Best wishes,

Kira

Kira Sinclair

BRING IT ON

TORONTO NEW YORK LONDON
AMSTERDAM PARIS SYDNEY HAMBURG
STOCKHOLM ATHENS TOKYO MILAN MADRID
PRAGUE WARSAW BUDAPEST AUCKLAND

Recycling programs
for this product may
not exist in your area.

ISBN-13: 978-0-373-79671-7

BRING IT ON

www.Harlequin.com

Printed in U.S.A.

ABOUT THE AUTHOR

When not working as an office manager for a project management firm or juggling plot lines, Kira spends her time on a small farm in north Alabama with her wonderful husband, two amazing daughters and a menagerie of animals. It's amazing to see how this self-proclaimed city girl has (or has not, depending on who you ask) adapted to country life. Kira enjoys hearing from her readers at her website, www.kirasinclair.com. Or stop by writingplayground. blogspot.com and join in the fight to stop the acquisition of an alpaca.

Books by Kira Sinclair

HARLEQUIN BLAZE
415—WHISPERS IN THE DARK
469—AFTERBURN
588—CAUGHT OFF GUARD
605—WHAT MIGHT HAVE BEEN

To get the inside scoop on Harlequin Blaze and its talented writers, be sure to check out blazeauthors.com.

All backlist available in ebook. Don't miss any of our special offers. Write to us at the following address for information on our newest releases.

Harlequin Reader Service
U.S.: 3010 Walden Ave., P.O. Box 1325, Buffalo, NY 14269
Canadian: P.O. Box 609, Fort Erie, Ont. L2A 5X3

I want to dedicate this book to my wonderful editor, Laura Barth. Not only is she a joy to work with, but her strengths are a perfect balance for my weaknesses. She helps me write the best book possible. Laura, here's definite proof that together we can figure anything out. Thank you!

_1_

"IF ANY MAN CAN SHOW just cause why this man and this woman should not be joined in holy matrimony, let him speak now or forever hold his peace."

Lena Fuller's stomach rolled as if she'd just gorged herself on junk food and then gotten on the worst roller coaster. Was it her imagination, or was every person inside the church holding their breath?

No, wait, that was just her.

But she wasn't imagining that everyone was staring at her. Although she supposed wearing a wedding dress made that a given.

She looked across at the man she was marrying. Wyn Rand. Flawless features. Aristocratic D.C. family. Challenging job. Limitless future.

Wyn was the perfect man for her. Nothing like the men her mother had paraded through her childhood. He respected her and appreciated her intelligence. He didn't treat her like a piece of meat, assuming the only thing she was good for was warming his bed.

All of her friends were jealous that she'd snagged

such a wonderful man. So why were the butterflies threatening to break through her stomach in a replay of *Alien?*

Her eyes drifted from Wyn with his pearly-white smile and confident gaze to the line of men standing diagonally behind him. Her gaze skipped purposely to Colt Douglas, one of her best friends.

He was three back in line, put there because she'd asked Wyn to include him in the wedding party. Wyn had never liked Colt, although Lena still didn't understand why. But Wyn had reluctantly acquiesced because it had been so important to her. She wanted—needed—Colt standing beside her on this important day.

She wasn't sure what she was looking for, maybe a smile of encouragement or a calm certainty she couldn't seem to find inside herself. It definitely wasn't the intense, laser-sharp stare Colt leveled at her. Nor the beginnings of a frown as the space between his brows wrinkled. Lena felt an answering pucker pull at her face.

No, wait, she should be smiling.

"I object." The small voice behind her quivered, but everyone heard the words anyway.

And suddenly Lena could breathe again.

Wyn's shocked gaze morphed into a glare that he directed somewhere over her shoulder. Something in the back of the church clattered loudly against the stone floor. The preacher sputtered, "Excuse me? I—I've never actually had anyone object."

No, probably not.

The preacher looked at her with a befuddled expression, as if she could tell him what to do next. As if this happened to her on a regular basis.

"I can't let you do this, Lena. I'm in love with Wyn. We've been having an affair for the last two months." Mitzi, her youngest aunt's oldest daughter, raced from the line of bridesmaids to stand between her and Wyn.

Lena focused in on her cousin's face. Peaches-and-cream beautiful, her eyes sparkling with the innocence of youth. An innocence she had no doubt this girl was about to lose. Wyn's mother was not going to be happy, and the woman was connected enough to make Mitzi's life hell. Lena tried to dredge up some sympathy for her but couldn't.

She watched mutely as Wyn attempted to pull Mitzi out from between them, to make her disappear, as if he could make the problem go away.

He hadn't even tried to deny it. And deep down, Lena wasn't surprised. Wyn didn't ask forgiveness of anyone...especially his future wife. Former future wife.

Mitzi leaned forward, straining against Wyn's hold. "I'm so sorry."

Yeah, right.

"I didn't mean for it to happen, Lena, honest. I ran into him at a club one weekend. We had a few drinks. One thing led to another."

Despite the shock and pressure suffusing her chest, Lena's own temper began to break through. How could this all be happening? On her wedding day.

"If you tell me he slipped and his dick fell into your vagina I'm going to strangle you."

A nervous titter went up from the congregation

beside her. Lena shot the entire mob a glare. Several of them stirred, the century-old wooden pews creaking beneath the weight of their guilty consciences.

"Mitzi, shut up." The first words Wyn bothered to speak and they were seriously less than helpful.

Around Lena chaos finally erupted. A cacophony of noise reached out to grab her. Pain burst through her chest when she looked into Wyn's eyes and realized that it was true. Guests talked to, at and above each other, making it difficult to pick out single voices from the crowd.

Her mother's high-pitched squeal, "I always said your daughter was a whore," joined her aunt's "At least she isn't a stuck-up snob who thinks she's better than everyone else."

Lena cringed at her aunt's words. She was not a snob. She just preferred not to associate with her mother's family. Frankly, they were all cut from the same self-absorbed, overly emotional cloth and she just didn't have the energy to deal with them. Putting up with her mother was draining enough.

Two of her cousins, Barley and Matthew, grabbed Mitzi's arms and tried to pull her away from the mass of people pouring up onto the steps of the sanctuary. Lena's best friends had rounded on the poor girl, their faces livid as they yelled at her for ruining Lena's wedding. And through it all, Wyn wouldn't let Mitzi go.

Lena stood in the center of it all, the motion and noise rushing past her, completely ignored.

Lena stared at her cousin. Nineteen. The girl was at

least eight years younger than Wyn. And in maturity and experience, he was light-years ahead.

A red haze filtered across Lena's vision. She closed the few steps that had separated her from Wyn and hauled back and slapped him. "Bastard."

Wyn looked stunned. Unfortunately, the livid red handprint across his cheek did nothing to dampen his perfect New England aristocratic good looks. For that, she hauled off and slapped him again.

Spinning on her heel, Lena tried to walk away, but the crowd of people pressed in around her. Her mother. Her cousin. Her best friends. Wyn. Wyn's mother. The people who moments ago had ignored her in favor of yelling at each other suddenly wouldn't let her leave.

Their fingers plucked at her. Someone stepped on her train. The dress had cost her six months' salary but had been worth every penny. She'd dreamed of what she would wear on this day ever since she was six, and the reality had been perfect. *Had* being the operative word.

The nasty sound of ripping satin and tulle made her cringe and the ping of crystal beads as they hit the marble floor made her want to scream. Her body jerked, straining against the phantom hold. And then she was blessedly free.

People, flower petals and sequins trailed in her wake as she raced down the aisle. She stumbled on the torn train, stopping long enough to scoop up the material and throw it over her elbow.

God, she must look a sight.

Her veil clouded around her face, obscuring her

vision and irritating the hell out of her. Lena reached up, yanked the thing off and threw it at someone as she flew by.

"Don't do anything rash, Lena. I'm sure you can work this out, dear," Diane, Wyn's mother, yelled behind her. The woman must really be panicked if she was willing to make that kind of public declaration. Diane was the perfect D.C. wife who spent her days organizing charitable events but didn't have an identity outside of her family and husband. Her face was frozen in place by too much Botox. Her hair was pulled back so tightly Lena wondered how the woman didn't have a permanent headache. And even on this day, her trademark single strand of pearls draped across the conservative neckline of her plum-colored dress.

That was what she'd almost signed up for. Relief washed over her.

But it was short-lived. Everywhere she looked there were people. Family, strangers, friends, enemies. All crying, yelling and full of pity.

She couldn't take it. It was all too much.

Pressing her hands over her ears, Lena looked for a way out.

She was halfway across the church when a calm in the center of the storm appeared. Colt stood beside the heavy wooden doors at the back of the church. His long and languid body was propped against the elegantly carved frame, both hands shoved into the pockets of his tux pants, one ankle crossed over the other as if he was just hanging out there, waiting.

He wasn't yelling. He wasn't freaking out.

She met his eyes, beautiful calm green eyes, so familiar and friendly. No pity or sorrow or anger or anything else, just Colt.

Relief pulsed beneath her skin, along with the urgent need to get out.

Her heels clicked against hard stone as she hurried toward Colt. Skidding to a halt, she looked into his eyes and said breathlessly, "Take me home."

"GET ME OUT OF THIS THING," she growled the minute her apartment door closed.

Not waiting for Colt to do as she'd asked, Lena craned her arms behind her, scrabbling at the tiny row of buttons running down the length of her spine. She struggled, twisting, trying in vain to reach them all and rid herself of the mountain of satin she'd crushed into the tiny passenger seat of his Porsche. That car definitely had not been made to hold two people and a wedding gown.

Brushing her fingers out of the way, Colt said, "Let me," and finished the job for her.

The slight tremor in her hands did not go unnoticed and Colt fought the urge—once again—to drive back to the church and beat the shit out of that sorry excuse for a man she'd almost married. The only thing that stopped him was knowing Lena wouldn't want him to make a scene. She hated drama. Never wanted to be the center of attention. While it would definitely make him feel better, it wouldn't do her any good.

He just hated to see her upset.

The bottom button had barely popped free before

she was pushing the voluminous mess off her shoulders and down her body. Pulling at the slip beneath, she left the lump of satin behind. Miraculously, it retained its shape, a sad white bell of material with a hole where her body should have been.

She blew out a sigh of relief, pushing the swell of her breasts against the edge of the full-length bra that skimmed over her hips and waist. Colt tried to ignore the way his mouth went dry, telling himself it was a normal male reaction to any woman undressing in front of him.

This was Lena. They'd been friends since they were kids. And if he'd occasionally woken from erotic dreams about her in the past, he told himself that it was simply the pitfall of having a female friend. Men thought about sex all the time, right? It was inevitable that his brain would put two and two together eventually.

Lena disappeared down the hallway. Deciding not to follow, Colt went into the kitchen and filled a wineglass from the open bottle he found in the fridge. It was the same bottle that had been there when he'd visited three months ago on his way to film a piece in Spain. He remembered because he'd come from Alaska where the frigid temperatures had played havoc with the film equipment. He'd brought the bottle with him, picking it up in the airport. He could no longer recall which airport it had been, they all started to look the same after a while.

Colt shook his head, hoping the wine hadn't spoiled. Yelling down the hall, he asked, "What now, Lee?"

She stuck her head around the corner, her bare shoulders just visible and her lips twisting into a crooked line. "I have no idea," she said before disappearing again.

Taking a sip of the chilled wine, he stopped in the open doorway of the kitchen, leaning against the jamb. The place was definitely bare. Lena had spent a lot of time and energy filling her apartment with things that mattered. It had been comfortable, warm and welcoming. This place had always been her pride and joy.

Boxes were stacked in the corner. He could see the neat labeling from here and knew she probably had a master list tucked into a binder cataloguing which box held what. The whole thing was depressing.

Lena returned wearing an oversize T-shirt and a pair of black leggings. Her hair, previously arranged into a twist that had probably taken hours, was now piled haphazardly on top of her head, tufts sticking out in every direction. In that moment she reminded him so much of the young girl he'd met so many years ago.

They'd both been ten the summer Lena and her mother moved into the estate next door. They'd become fast friends, inseparable. She'd spent more time at his house than hers, blending seamlessly into his family. His parents had treated her like one of their own.

When she'd left nine months later he'd been so upset. His parents had given Lena a laptop so they could keep in touch. And they had, building a friendship on emails, phone calls and brief visits here and there that had lasted through distance and time.

He hadn't seen that carefree girl in a very long time.

He wasn't sure when she'd disappeared—probably when her mother was dragging her all over the world. Or maybe after his parents' fatal accident. His life had been falling apart and she'd been holding together the pieces for him. Or possibly while he was rushing from one corner of the globe to another, working his butt off trying to prove his talents as a photographer and documentarian were more important than his bank account and family name.

Sure, he could have bought a production company and hired himself to direct any film he wanted, but that wouldn't prove he had the skills to make it on his own.

Staring at Lena, he wondered what else he'd missed in the months and years they'd been separated. And whether he could have prevented the debacle at the church if he'd been here more than a few days at a time.

Closing the space between them, he held out the wine he'd poured for her. With a sad smile, she took a long swallow. Cradling the glass against her body, her mouth twisted over the rim. "I think it's going to take more than some wine to fix this one."

Unfortunately she was right, and her family would likely descend at any moment. "This probably isn't the best place to hide. Maybe you should get away for a few days?" he suggested. "Let things die down a bit before you have to deal with everything."

"I can't afford to go anywhere. I spent all my savings on the dress." She gestured halfheartedly to the pile of satin still sitting behind them in the entranceway.

"What about the honeymoon?"

"Wyn paid for it," she said slowly, drawing out the

words as she apparently turned over the idea. "But I've got all of the travel documents."

For the first time since he'd walked into the church, Colt felt a genuine smile tug at his lips. "Even better. Where was he going to take you?"

A spark flickered in her eyes for just a moment as she told him, "To a secluded Caribbean resort off the coast of St. Lucia. It's supposed to be upscale, adults only. I was really looking forward to it."

"Well then, I think it's the least the bastard owes you."

"No, I can't. Besides, I wouldn't want to go by myself. That would just be…depressing."

"So take a friend."

Lena's head cocked to the side as she studied him for several moments. "What are you doing for the next week?"

"No, I didn't mean me," he sputtered.

"Why not? I haven't seen you in forever. The last time you were in town hardly counts. You were so jet-lagged you spent half your time sleeping."

Colt could see the hope in Lena's eyes. He hated to disappoint her. "I was hoping to be in Peru to film a documentary about an exciting archaeological find, but the producer chose another director."

"I'm so sorry, Colt. I know you really wanted to land that one. Why didn't you tell me when you found out?"

"You were all wrapped up in the wedding plans. Besides, it isn't important. Something else will come along. It always does."

He tried to hide his disappointment, but probably

failed miserably. The job was perfect, everything he'd been working and waiting for. A great opportunity, an interesting subject and a challenging location.

Lena didn't seem to pick up on his lie, though; she was understandably preoccupied with her own disappointment.

"So there's no reason you can't go with me. Come on. Fruity drinks and lounge chairs on the beach. Sleeping late, five-star meals. You know you want to."

He opened his mouth to say no again, but as her eyes went misty with unshed tears, Colt realized it was a losing battle. When she said, "Please, Colt, I need you," it was the final nail in his coffin.

"Fine." He sighed, and tried to ignore the tremble of her bottom lip when she wrapped her arms around his body and squeezed tight.

"Thank you," she whispered against his skin, her nose buried in the crook of his neck.

Her breath tickled and something thick tightened in the back of his throat. He ignored it.

He held her, knowing what she needed right now more than anything was a friend. But the moment was interrupted when a loud knock sounded on the door.

"Lena, let me in." A man's voice boomed through the closed door.

Colt didn't have to ask who was on the other side. The stiffening of Lena's muscles beneath the circle of his arms said it all.

Jerking away from him, she faced the door, but didn't actually move to open it. "Go away, Wyn. I don't want to talk to you right now."

"Fine, but your mother gave me your suitcase."

Lena cursed under her breath. "Of course she did. Remind me to thank her." She rolled her eyes and grimaced. "Right after I kill her."

Shaking her head, Lena headed for the door. Colt reached out to stop her, but she was too fast. "You don't have to let him in."

"I do if I want any clothes to wear on the island. I wonder how long it took my mother to realize she could hand Wyn the perfect excuse to make me see him."

Not long, Colt guessed. The woman was flighty, but she was also calculating. From everything Lena had told him about her childhood—which wasn't much— he'd gathered her mother had spent her entire life moving from man to man—and dragging Lena behind her. Her only valuable skills seemed to be charming and wheedling her way into whatever she wanted.

The minute Lena opened the door, Wyn pushed past her. However, he slammed to a halt the minute he saw Colt. With a dark scowl on his face, he said, "What's he doing here?"

Colt knew Wyn had never liked him, but then the feeling had been mutual, so he didn't exactly hold that against him. What he did have a problem with was the way he'd treated Lena.

She deserved better.

"Give me one good reason. That's all I need," Colt promised in a calm and even voice, taking a menacing step towards him.

Lena inserted herself in the middle, splitting a hard

stare between them. Tension simmered as they both glared across the top of Lena's head.

"Stop it, both of you."

Wyn took a step forward, but she planted her hand hard into the center of his chest, stopping him in his tracks. The minute her palm collided with him, she recoiled. A knowing smirk touched Colt's lips and he enjoyed the way Wyn's mouth tightened into a hard line.

"Thanks for returning my suitcase. You can go now."

Wyn tried to reach for her, but she scooted backward, straight into Colt. For a minute she jerked the other way, but as soon as her mind caught up and she realized he wasn't a threat, she leaned gratefully against the solid line of his body.

"Lena, we need to talk," Wyn said, grinding the words out between clenched teeth.

"I have nothing to say."

"Okay, then just listen."

"I don't want to hear it. All I want is for you to leave."

"Look, we still have the honeymoon. Why don't we go away? See if we can fix this. I mean, see if I can fix this."

Lena shook her head, sadness clouding her eyes. Colt wanted to rush to her defense, to stand between them both and defend her, but he realized she didn't need his help. She was perfectly capable of handling this on her own. She'd always been a strong woman—it was something he admired about her.

"I'm not going anywhere with you. I am, however, taking the trip that you promised me. I think it's the least that you owe me. A chance to get away, sort through some things. Maybe after I get back I'll be ready to talk to you, but don't think for a second that means I'll ever take you back. I experienced enough dysfunctional, toxic relationships with my mother. I have no intention of falling into one myself."

A hard glint entered Wyn's eyes. He wasn't happy, but then there wasn't much he could do about it. What did it say about Colt that he delighted in seeing the other man thwarted?

"What if I just show up?"

"I wouldn't do that if I were you. Besides, I'm not going alone. Colt is coming with me."

Wyn's body bowed tight with anger. Colt had no doubt that it was barely in check. Taking a deliberate step forward, Colt drew Wyn's glittering gaze.

"I always knew there was something more between you two."

Lena let out an exasperated sound, as if this was ground they'd covered more than once and she was sick of traveling it. "How many times do I have to tell you? There's nothing between us. Hell, I barely see him. Don't paint me with your brush just because you're feeling guilty at being caught."

Wyn's teeth ground together. Colt could hear them from where he stood several feet away. If the man had come here to beg forgiveness, he certainly had an ass-backward way of doing it. But Colt had no intention of pointing that out.

"Fine. Enjoy your trip." Looking Colt square in the eyes, Wyn said, "I hope you get sunburned."

Colt delighted in being able to smile at him and promise, "Don't worry about me. I never burn. And I swear I'll keep Lena good and covered up. Or even better, out of the sun altogether. I wonder what else there is to do on a romantic tropical island besides swim?"

2

THE LAST TWENTY-FOUR HOURS had been hell. Sure, Colt had upgraded them both to first class but a delayed flight, two hours sitting on the tarmac, a missed connection and nine hours in the Atlanta airport were not how she'd envisioned the trip beginning. Of course, nothing about the past day had happened as planned.

But they were here now and that was what mattered.

The island was about forty-five minutes by ferry from St. Lucia. The ride over had been amazing—bright blue sky, therapeutic sunshine and a brisk tropical breeze that had helped to clear the jetlag cobwebs from her brain.

When Wyn had told her he'd booked them at Escape, Lena had checked the place out online. The resort, the only thing on Île du Coeur, had a volatile and romantic history. The small island had originally been a cocoa plantation but had been turned into a boutique resort about fifty years ago. It had been renovated, added onto, changed hands multiple times and let fall into disrepair until the current owner had purchased it almost three years ago. The place was now billed as an adult-only tropical retreat. Small and intimate, lush and seductive, perfect for a honeymoon.

Apparently, there was a local legend to the name of the place. *Île du Coeur* literally translated meant Heart Island. Supposedly, everyone who visited found their heart's desire—whether it was what they were looking for or not. Lena had her doubts, but she had to admit that it was a great marketing angle.

Lena had been surprised that Wyn had sprung for the most expensive bungalow at an already pricey resort. The man came from money, but he was very careful about how he spent it. His frugal nature was one of the things that had attracted her to Wyn in the first place. Considering where she'd come from, that quality had been extremely important to Lena.

Her mother had been…erratic. Hell, she was still unreliable. Using her ethereal beauty and fragility, she'd spent her life conning a succession of men into taking care of her. But the arrangement was never permanent. It had been a good year if Lena didn't have to change schools more than once. And that was assuming her mother actually enrolled her. Sure, she'd lived in Europe, Brazil, D.C., New York and possibly every state in between, and she'd hated every last second of it. Except for those few months with Colt and his family. That was the only time she'd ever felt that she belonged.

All she'd ever wanted was to find someplace permanent, to grow some roots. Someplace that wouldn't change in the middle of the night when the wife discovered the mistress, and Lena and her mother were thrown out on their ear.

The only contact she'd ever had from her father was the monthly check that provided the only steady income they had. Unfortunately, it wasn't enough to keep her mother in the lifestyle she preferred. Lena had often wondered if her mother had gotten pregnant on purpose, just to ensure money would come from somewhere. She'd never been brave enough to ask. Probably because she'd been afraid of what the answer might be.

Normally Lena wouldn't have been one to splurge on unnecessary luxuries, but whatever Wyn had spent on the honeymoon had been worth every penny.

The island was gorgeous, just what she'd expected. Lush colors—green grass, red, pink and yellow flowers, rough brown trunks of towering palm trees and clear turquoise water—surrounded her. The pebbled path leading from the pier to the main building wound through perfect landscaping. She could hear laughter and music floating on the warm sultry air.

The grand facade of the plantation house greeted them. Antique wood and faded walls lent an aura of old-world charm and history that just couldn't be faked. A larger more modern building rose up behind the house. No doubt it had been added at some point to expand the hotel space.

Lena spun on the path trying to take it all in as Colt held the door open for her. Ducking beneath his outstretched arm, she scooted past. The minute her body brushed against his, an unexpected tension stole into her limbs. It wasn't the first time she'd had this kind of reaction to Colt, although it had been a while. She groaned inwardly. Why did the physical reaction always have to blindside her? It was nothing. Chemistry. Shaking it off, she tried to focus on the lobby.

Polished wooden floors, hand-carved molding and period fabrics covering the chairs all gave the space an air of authenticity that immediately charmed her. From across the room a cheerful woman with friendly eyes asked, "Checking in?"

Lena nodded, the first genuine smile she'd felt in days on her face. "Lena Fuller."

"Rand," Colt's deep voice rumbled behind her.

She whipped her head around to look at him. "What?"

"I imagine they'd have you listed under Rand, not Fuller."

Lena wrinkled her nose. "I suppose so."

"Oh, are you the Rands?"

"No—"

"Not rea—"

The cheerful woman spoke over their words, moving away as she said, "We've been expecting you, although we thought you were arriving on the earlier ferry. Let me get Marcy for you, she'll be handling everything while you're here."

Not only was she friendly, but fast. The woman disappeared, leaving Lena standing at the vacant counter, her mouth hanging open, unsaid words stuck in her throat. Colt tapped his finger on her chin and she snapped her jaws shut, ignoring the rush of heat that blasted through her face.

A small woman burst through the doorway behind the wooden counter. Beautiful pale hair fluttered around the sharp angles of her face. She carried her shoulders in the straight line of a drill sergeant, telling Lena that she was definitely in charge.

Marcy stuck her hand out and Lena automatically grasped it.

"Welcome to Escape. I'm Marcy."

She reached for Colt's hand. "It's nice to finally meet you in person, Wyn. Of course, I'll be working with you both this week, trying to keep everything flowing smoothly."

"Working?" Lena's mind raced, but she couldn't make sense of what Marcy was saying.

"The production crew arrived yesterday and set up this morning. We were under the impression you'd be arriving earlier, but I suppose things happen when you're traveling."

Lena found herself apologizing, although she wasn't exactly sure why. Normally, hotels didn't care when you checked in and none of the literature she'd read about Escape indicated there was a strict policy. "We missed a connection."

"No matter. We're on a tight schedule, but we've adjusted things accordingly. The team would like to start immediately with some romantic shots during your welcome dinner this evening once you've settled."

The fireball glanced down at the tiny gold watch wrapped around her slender wrist. "Your reservations are at seven so that gives you a couple hours to settle into your bungalow and unpack." With a smile that was more perfunctory than welcoming, she asked, "Any questions?"

"Yes, what are you talking about?" Lena stared blankly at Marcy. It was as if she was speaking another language, one Lena knew she should understand but didn't.

"The photo shoot." The other woman's eyes glanced behind her at Colt before returning to Lena again. "Surely Wyn explained everything to you."

Colt cleared his throat. "Perhaps you could do us both a favor and go over it again."

An expression of disbelief and irritation flitted across Marcy's face, but she looked at Lena and explained. "Wyn and I have been working on a marketing campaign for Escape. When we started throwing around the idea of featuring a couple, he had the brilliant suggestion that we use you both as a real example of a loving couple honeymooning on our beautiful island."

"Why would we want to spend our honeymoon posing for an ad campaign?"

Marcy's brow wrinkled as her frown deepened. "Because you aren't paying for the vacation." She shot another nasty look across at Colt. "He really didn't tell you any of this?"

"No, no, he didn't."

"I'm going to kill him." Colt's words were low and she thought Marcy hadn't actually heard them. He started to turn, but Lena grasped his arm and held him there beside her. His biceps flexed beneath her hand. When had he gotten so strong?

"Where do you think you're going?"

"To catch the first ferry so I can kick his ass. He could have stopped us or told us, but he didn't. Don't worry, I'll be back before you know it."

Frowning at him, she said, "That isn't funny," before directing her attention back to Marcy who now looked just as confused as Lena had been moments ago.

"Marcy, there's been a mix-up."

"You aren't Lena Rand?"

"No, yes, I mean I'm Lena but—"

"Are you telling me that if we don't go through with the photo shoot that we can't stay at the resort?" Colt raised his voice to drown out the rest of her words.

"Yes. No. Why would you want to back out now?" Marcy's gaze bored into Colt's. "You signed a contract, Wyn."

"Um, I didn't get married and this isn't Wyn," Lena blurted out. She almost felt sorry for Marcy as her eyes widened with shock before narrowing into slits.

"What do you mean this isn't Wyn? What the hell is going on?"

Lena swallowed, realizing it was the first time she'd had to say out loud what had happened since leaving the church. "Let's just say that Wyn decided he preferred my teenage whore of a cousin."

Marcy blinked owlishly and then waved her hand in Colt's direction. "Then who is this?"

"A friend," she said, before realizing just how that might sound.

Marcy's eyes narrowed just a little more as she took

in the sight of Lena, unmarried Lena, with Colt towering over her in that way of his.

Lena launched a preemptive strike. "No, seriously, we're just friends. When the wedding fell apart Colt was there. I had the honeymoon, or what I thought was supposed to be a honeymoon, and we hadn't seen each other in a very long time." Lena realized she was rambling but couldn't seem to stop herself. "He travels. He's a director. He makes documentaries all over the world."

"Well, isn't that nice for him," Marcy said, looking unconvinced.

"How much would a week here cost, Marcy?" Colt asked, filling the pregnant silence. Which was a good thing because who knew what might come out of Lena's mouth if she opened it again.

"We reserved the honeymoon bungalow for Wyn, the best location on property. An entire week there would cost $8,595. Not including tax."

"It's a private island. How can there be tax?" Colt asked.

"We have to pay the mainland for use of their utilities, municipal resources and the ferry service. But price isn't the problem."

Tension poured off Colt in waves. Lena could feel it tightening the muscles in her own back. He was frustrated, angry and ready to kill someone; the only problem was that the target for his anger was an entire ocean away. Normally, she wasn't a violent person, but if Wyn had been standing next to them, she most definitely would have let Colt have at him. She was getting angrier and angrier with her ex-fiancé by the minute.

"Then what is the problem?" she asked.

"We're booked solid. I don't have another available room for four days. I have a contract with the production company, a deadline with the ad agency and an internationally distributed travel magazine. I don't need more paying guests, I need a couple to photograph for our ad campaign."

With a dismayed glance behind her, Marcy looked at Colt. She wasn't sure why. It wasn't his job to fix the mess Wyn had created.

"So basically, you're saying our choices are to agree to appear in your photo shoot and get a free vacation or leave?"

For a moment, Lena thought she saw a glimmer of panic and regret flash through the other woman's eyes, but before she could pounce it was gone.

"Look, I'm sorry, but I'm stuck between a rock and a hard place. You're both attractive. You'd make a great couple for our ad campaign. If you're willing to do the work, I'd be happy to give you the same agreement I offered Wyn. Free room, food and amenities in exchange for your cooperation with our photography team."

Lena looked around her at the charmingly elegant lobby. Outside the windows she could see the beckoning water and almost hear the lap of the waves as they hit the sand.

She didn't want to leave. Not yet. Her life back home was a shambles. She wasn't ready to face it. The resort was beautiful. She'd been looking forward to staying.

"I suppose it could be worse," she said, looking back at Colt and raising one eyebrow in reluctant surrender.

"How?"

"I could have actually married Wyn."

A laugh rumbled deep in Colt's chest. Lena was close enough to feel the vibrations and found an answering smile touch her lips.

"I suppose it would be an adventure. How much work could it possibly be? We're here…" His voice trailed off. Even he seemed reluctant to turn around immediately and leave. And considering what an ordeal it had been to get here, Lena didn't blame him. The thought of getting back on a plane right now was not appealing. Especially when she had sandy beaches and a crystal-clear sea stretching invitingly in front of her.

Marcy's relieved smile was hard to miss. "I guess the only question that remains—since you insist that you're not a couple—is can the two of you pull off looking like honeymooners for the cameras?"

"Please. I've spent most of my adult life behind the camera, plotting angles and setting up shots. I think I can handle being in front of it."

Without any warning, Colt grasped Lena's upper arm and spun her around to face him. She wobbled a little, until his arms around her body steadied her. What was he doing?

Laughter still lingered in the back of his bright green eyes. A soft smile touched his mouth, curving his lips even as they parted, moved closer. Lena found her own lips drifting apart. What was *she* doing?

He bent her backward over his arm, making the

room and her equilibrium tilt. His mouth claimed hers in a devastating kiss. She had a moment of shock when her body went rigid, but it was quickly overwhelmed by a radiating warmth that melted through her bones.

He didn't devour her as some men had a habit of doing. He gently persuaded her to open to him, constant pressure and reassurance that he wouldn't push beyond what she was comfortable giving.

After several seconds…or maybe minutes, he slowly, smoothly, pulled her back upright and let her go. The world tilted around her for a few seconds.

Her lungs burned. She took a deep breath to fill them back up again, but instead of the tropical scent permeating the lobby, all she could smell now was Colt. A masculine scent that always made her think of sandalwood.

What the hell had just happened?

"Satisfied?" Colt's voice was smooth and poised. Unaffected. While Lena wasn't sure she could actually form coherent words. She blinked, trying to clear her vision and the shift her world had taken.

She'd always known he was a good kisser. While he never kept a girl around long, she'd had occasion to mingle with a few of his conquests. They'd always been quick to sing his praises, as if they had some shared knowledge. No one ever believed her when she said they'd never slept together.

Marcy arched an eyebrow, pursed her lips and considered them for several seconds. "I suppose that settles that. Welcome to Escape."

3

WHY HAD HE KISSED HER?

It had seemed like a harmless thing to do at the time—take a little dig at Marcy and show her she had nothing to worry about—right up until the moment his lips had touched Lena's. He'd expected it to be light, quick, unimportant. Somehow between the idea and the execution, it had all gone wrong. Instead of something theatrical, he'd found himself really kissing her.

He'd pressed in slowly and asked her for more. And she'd given it. He wasn't sure what was more shocking, his reaction or hers.

The gut-deep wrench of yearning had come out of nowhere. Left him breathless and reeling. It'd taken everything he had inside to let her go. To pretend nothing had happened. Nothing had changed.

But it had.

He'd known her for sixteen years. When they were children it had been easy, connecting mostly through emails and phone calls. They'd skipped the awkward exploration of teenage years because she was always so far away. And while they'd both gone to college in D.C., they'd been at different schools. They'd seen each other more often, but not every day. They'd always lived separate lives and it was easy to continue to do that even in the same city.

And then his parents had died and he'd...floundered. His brother had tried to fill the void, but he had a young family to take care of. Lena was there for him, and he'd needed her so much. Needed the steady support of their friendship. It was the only thing that had felt real and solid when the rest of his life had spun out of control.

D.C. had become a constant reminder of the parents he'd lost. The family home. His brother, sister-in-law and newborn niece. He'd begun taking jobs, going anywhere as a way to escape it all. However, the work had quickly become important to him for other reasons. He enjoyed the challenges that came with difficult projects and the transient lifestyle that allowed him to move from place to place, constantly experiencing something new.

Ahead of him on the path, Lena's bright voice floated back to him. "Ooh, they have snorkeling. Maybe Marcy will let us do that one afternoon."

It was a fluke. That was all. This was Lena they were talking about. They'd studied together, shared pizza, razzed each other about horrible taste in movies, spent hours on the phone when he called from faraway places. She'd been there for him during the worst possible moments of his life.

She'd been the first person at the hospital the night he'd crashed his car going one-twenty down a back-country road. She'd tried to talk him out of skydiving, base jumping and extreme rock climbing. But when he'd refused to listen, she'd been there to bandage his cuts and smack the back of his head. Ultimately, she was the one who shook him out of his grief over losing his parents and convinced him he needed to get back to living.

Lena was important.

Sure, they rarely saw each other now—for the past five years he'd been wandering the globe trying to make his mark as a filmmaker—but their friendship was easy. They could go weeks or even months without talking, but when he did pick up the phone, it was as if they'd spoken the night before.

He didn't want to lose that. He needed her grounding influence in his life.

Gritting his teeth, Colt determined to ignore the firestorm of hormones raging inside his body until it went away. She'd just been jilted, for heaven's sake. The last thing she needed was to deal with his wayward lust. And really, that's all it was. A quick reaction based on a bad decision. He'd been so busy on his last job in Kenya that he hadn't had time to blow off steam.

Eventually, it would subside and things would go back to normal. Until then, he could fake it.

"Ooh," she said again, stopping short on the path. Skidding to a halt, he barely missed colliding with her.

She looked up at the tiny bungalow Marcy had assigned them, although he supposed *tiny* was a relative term. As a permanent residence it would never have done. But as vacation spots went it was pretty amazing.

The outside was made of warm, polished wood that gleamed beneath the late-afternoon sun. Lena pushed open the solid door, revealing the dark interior. Cool air leaked out to touch Colt's skin. Before that moment, he hadn't realized how hot it was here.

Their bags, along with an itinerary Marcy was eager to get started on, were to be delivered shortly. In the meantime, they had nothing to do but explore their temporary home.

Lena was busy wandering around the edges of the room, looking through the windows and squealing about their private infinity pool on their secluded patio.

All he could see was the single king-size four-poster bed that dominated half the room.

Eventually, Lena made her way over to it. She bounced down onto the mattress, the comforter bunching up around her and the pillows toppling haphazardly behind her.

"One bed, huh. Wanna draw straws?"

"Please. You're welcome to take the couch if you don't trust yourself in the same bed with me," he joked, a smile plastered to his still-pulsing lips.

She snorted. "It's my honeymoon. If anyone's sleeping on the couch, it's you." She flopped onto her back, her arms spread wide across the entire length of the bed. "It would be the gentlemanly thing to do."

"You've known me for how long?"

"Long enough."

"So you know better than to accuse me of being a gentleman."

"True enough." She laughed. Sitting up, she looked across at him.

"Why did you do that?"

He thought he knew what she was talking about, but part of him hoped he was wrong. "Do what?"

Her mouth took on a serious slant. "Kiss me."

He shrugged. "It seemed like a good idea at the time."

Awkwardness, never present before, settled between them. He realized that he should probably apologize. Or maybe promise her he wouldn't do it again. But the words didn't form.

"Well, um, let's try to avoid having to do that again."

"Well, hell, I've never gotten any complaints before." He exaggerated his words, pulling his face into a mock scowl, trying to restore the equilibrium they'd lost. "Was kissing me such a hardship?"

"I didn't say that."

"You enjoyed it."

"I didn't say that, either," she exclaimed, rolling her eyes.

"Anyway, I don't think Marcy will require that kind of commitment. From either of us." He hoped.

"Maybe not, but I'd really like to avoid having to explain to everyone what happened. I'm here to forget about the wedding, and I'm afraid these photo sessions will cause a stir. Maybe we should just pretend that we're actually married."

Well, he definitely hadn't expected this. But, now that he thought about it, her suggestion made sense. If he were in her position, he wouldn't want to have to retell the story over and over, reliving the painful experience.

"All right," he agreed slowly. "I have a problem with outright lying, but I don't mind letting people think whatever they want."

"Thank you," she said softly.

A knock at the door signaled the arrival of their luggage and put an end to their conversation. Several minutes later, he found himself outside walking slowly around the rim of the pool while Lena got ready for their first assignment—a romantic dinner, according to Marcy.

He just hoped he could get through the night without doing something he'd regret. Like kissing her again.

AWKWARDNESS HAD SETTLED around them again. The restaurant was elegant and romantic, which probably didn't help the situation. Decorated in soft blues and greens that complemented the untamed tropical beauty outside, the dining area had an undercurrent of sensuality and sophistication. It was the sort of place a man took a woman he was planning to seduce, Lena thought.

Her eyes strayed sideways to Colt as the maître d' led them through the restaurant. Colt's hand settled lightly on the small of her back, guiding her through the maze of tables. Her muscles tightened beneath his touch, making her feel even more unsettled.

Colt had touched her a thousand times. Hadn't he? Her body had never responded this way before. Had it?

Lena thought hard. Maybe. When they were both in college, there'd been some faint wisp of attraction.

But it had gone away, to be replaced by deep affection. Which meant more than a fleeting physical attraction that could burn out and die. Right?

She'd seen it time and time again growing up. Her mother would gush over the latest man in her life. Her cheeks would be pink, her eyes would glow. But three months later there would be yelling and crying. Until the next man and the next place. If Lena had learned anything from watching her mother, it was that sexual attraction never lasted and was hardly the foundation for a good relationship.

Oh, she liked sex just as much as the next woman, but she'd always looked for more than a spark. Which is what she'd thought she'd found with Wyn.

The sommelier approached their table and introduced himself. "Marcy has arranged for a flight of excellent wines to accompany your dinner this evening." Twisting the bottle he'd held against his arm, he presented it to Colt for his inspection. "This is our best champagne, compliments of the house in celebration of your marriage."

Colt, who had leaned forward, sprawled back into his chair. The tip of his shoe nudged against her foot. Lena drew her own feet back underneath her chair. Two days ago, heck two hours ago, it wouldn't have bothered her. But something had changed. An awareness of him as a man had sprung up seemingly out of nowhere.

Oh, she'd always thought he was an attractive man. With his rugged good looks and the well-defined muscles his dangerous hobbies had given him, any woman would be hard-pressed to argue. Colt had an air about him, an adventurous spirit that made you think you'd never be bored while he was around.

But she didn't want adventure, never had. She wanted a man who would settle in one place, build a solid and stable life for her and their children. Colt didn't fit that bill. Yet another reason she'd never thought of him in a romantic or sexual way.

"Didn't you hear? We're not—"

Lena kicked him with her sandal-clad foot, stubbing her toe and shutting him up in one fell swoop. Grimacing, she said, "Colt, behave."

"What would be the fun in that?" he asked, mischief glinting in his eyes. She'd seen that look before, many times, and it usually heralded some harebrained scheme that she wanted no part of—such as jumping out of a perfectly functioning airplane.

There were many things about Colt that she liked. He was a good friend, always there for her when she needed him. But there was plenty about him that she just didn't understand, and she had convinced herself a long time ago she never would.

She shot Colt a warning look for good measure as the sommelier poured. Lena gratefully accepted her glass. Taking a sip, she let the chilled bubbles tickle her nose and cascade down her throat. "Mmm, this is good." It was light and fruity, sweet on her tongue. She took another sip. And another.

Looking at Colt, she smiled. Candlelight flickered between them, casting shifting shadows across his face. She wanted to reach out and run the pad of her finger over his skin. Her smile vanished and her eyes darted away. What was she thinking? She lifted her glass and drained it.

Colt palmed the bottle from the waiting bucket and asked, "More?"

The playful mask he'd been wearing slipped and for the first time Lena realized he was worried about her. The space between his eyebrows wrinkled and his lips pulled tight into a straight line.

"I'm fine," she said.

Colt shrugged, the dress shirt he'd put on pulling tight against the broad expanse of his shoulders. "If you say so."

She was halfway through her second glass, on an empty stomach, when Marcy appeared at her elbow.

"All settled in?"

Lena looked up at the other woman, at the strained smile that stretched her lips but didn't touch her eyes.

"Yes, the bungalow is lovely."

"I'm so glad you're pleased."

Marcy plunked something that made a metallic twang onto the table. The plain gold bands rattled for a moment before settling against each other. "I noticed you didn't have rings. We'll need them for the photographs."

Lena stared at the rings. Without looking at her, Colt reached for the bigger one, slipping it onto his finger.

She swallowed, picked hers up and slid it snugly against the princess-cut diamond already on her finger. She'd been wearing the engagement ring for so long she'd forgotten it was there. Now, however, it felt all wrong, and she wished she'd left it back in D.C. Both bands sat heavy against her skin. She didn't want either of them, but when Marcy let out a sigh of relief, Lena dropped her hands into her lap, her naked right covering her left.

With a wave of her hand, Marcy pulled over a man with a camera draped across his neck. Lena had wondered when the three-ring circus would start.

"This is Mikhail. He's going to be the photographer this week. The photo shoot was supposed to be organic, catching a real honeymooning couple as they explored all the resort had to offer. We were hoping to use candid shots. Obviously, that might be a little difficult now."

"Why do you say that?" Colt asked.

Marcy shot him an incredulous look. "Well, for starters, you're both sitting as far away from each other as possible without being at separate tables."

Colt's lips dipped down into a frown. Lena took in their positions and realized Marcy was right. A hard glint entered Colt's eyes. Slapping his hand down onto the table, his open palm waited expectantly as he said, "Give me your hand."

Reluctantly, Lena placed her hand in his. His fingers brushed against the pulse at her wrist, sending it skittering. A warm heat that had nothing to do with the alcohol she'd drunk suffused her skin.

Colt's eyes changed, going from hard to soft. He pulled their joined hands closer, forcing her to either let go or press her body against the biting edge of the table.

She'd left her hair down and it fell around her face, somehow closing the rest of the restaurant out and training her focus solely on him. Colt leaned forward, meeting her halfway across the table. His tongue licked across his lips, drawing her attention to his mouth. She'd never bothered to study it before. Or maybe it had been intentional avoidance. But since he'd used his mouth against her...

It was sensual, wide. The dip in the center of his top lip flared out in a way that made her want to close the gap between them and suck it into her own mouth.

Something flared in the back of his eyes. An awareness and intensity she'd only ever seen him focus on someone else.

She leaned closer. The candle burning between them flickered with the breeze from their joined breaths.

What was she doing?

Her teeth clinked together and she pulled back. He reluctantly let her hand go. His palm scraped slowly against hers. Her nerve endings pulsed and flared, sending unwanted signals all through her body.

Lena put her hands in her lap and rubbed her palm, trying to stop the ripple effect. It didn't work. The damage was already done. She blinked, feeling sluggish, disoriented and sorely out of her element.

"Better?" he asked in a low rumbling voice that sent shivers down her spine.

Without thought, Lena nodded, and then realized Colt was no longer looking at her but up at Marcy.

"Uh-huh," Marcy uttered before clearing her throat and jerking her gaze away. "Mikhail, we'll try the candid shots tonight."

Marcy flicked them one more calculating glance

before melting away from their table. Lena thought she heard the other woman whisper, "Wine. Lots of wine," to their sommelier as she passed, but she couldn't be certain.

Lena looked across at Colt and for the first time in their friendship had no idea what to say. Luckily, the salad course arrived and saved her from having to come up with something.

Her mouth watered at the crisp greens, strawberries, candied nuts and light citrus dressing their waiter placed before her. She was grateful for something to occupy her hands...and her mouth.

But apparently Colt wasn't as desperate for the distraction. He took a few bites and then set his fork down. Instead of eating, he watched her. Several times she picked up her napkin and blotted her lips for fear that the dressing was dribbling down her chin. She was already on edge and he wasn't helping any. She was about to tell him to knock it off, but he spoke before her.

"Why did you want to marry Wyn?"

Surprised by his question, she sputtered for a few seconds, unsure what to say. They'd never really talked about her relationship with Wyn before. She didn't know why, but there was some tacit agreement between them. He didn't tell her about the women who flitted through his life and she rarely mentioned Wyn when they spoke.

It felt weird to be talking with Colt about him now, but he'd asked. She tried to remember exactly what it was about Wyn that had mattered. Her brain felt fuzzy and the only thing she could come up with was, "Because...he was good to me."

"Not because you loved him."

"Of course I loved him," Lena protested.

Colt shook his head. "I don't think there's any 'of course' about it. You haven't even cried."

"I hate crying in front of people. You know that," she scoffed, dismissing his statement without really even thinking about it.

"Maybe. But I watched you up on that altar. You were so pale I was worried you might faint. Right up until the minute your cousin objected and then color flooded your cheeks. You were shocked, possibly angry, but that was relief I saw all over your face."

Lena looked at him, the pleasant buzz that had entered her blood lessening just a little. Was he right?

"You're upset because things didn't work out the way you wanted them to. Maybe you're even embarrassed that it fell apart in front of so many people." Colt paused. "But you aren't heartbroken."

He was wrong. Wasn't he? "How is heartbroken supposed to look, Colt? Am I supposed to be inconsolable? Sobbing in my bed surrounded by spent tissues? Please. I've seen that scene before, more times than I care to count."

Her tongue felt loose, unhinged. Even as she said the words, she realized she was sharing more with him than she meant to. More than she'd ever said before. To anyone. "Do you know how often I scraped together the pieces of my mother and tried to put them back together? How many times I had to beg and plead with her just to get out of bed? After every man—there were plenty and they all left—she'd spend days, weeks, sometimes months inconsolable and incapable of doing anything. Especially taking care of a child."

She glared across at him, years of conviction radiating from her eyes. "I refuse to be like her. I will not let a relationship devastate or control me like that. So, yes, I'm upset. Wyn and I were supposed to have a life together. He betrayed me in the worst possible way. With my cousin. Excuse me if I'm not handling the situation the way you expected me to."

Colt's eyes were round with shock. His silence slammed down between them and the minute it did Lena regretted her words. It was obvious that he'd gotten way more than he'd bargained for.

Their food hadn't even arrived, but that didn't matter. Lena wasn't hungry anymore. In fact, she needed to get out of there before she said even more. Lena scraped her chair against the stone floor and walked toward the exit.

Colt called her name. The photographer cursed.

She ignored them both.

4

COLT HEARD THE MAN CURSE, too, and couldn't have agreed more. How was he to know his question would hit a sore spot? They were supposed to be friends, right?

Lena had seen him at his absolute worst. When he'd crashed his car, she'd been the one to sit by him in the hospital. He'd told her things about his life that he'd never shared with anyone else. She'd seen him cry, moan with pain and had supported him even when she thought he was making unwise decisions.

How could there be part of her life he knew nothing about? Why had she never told him how bad her mother had been?

Thinking back on those months she'd lived next door, he realized they'd rarely gone to her house. When he'd asked, she'd almost always had an excuse. Sure, he'd only been ten, but why hadn't he picked up on that? And why, in all the times that they'd talked since then, had she not shared her pain? Heaven knew he'd dumped plenty of his own worries on her small, capable shoulders.

The table teetered, silverware, china and glass clinking ominously, as he bolted after her.

Tropical heat and guilt slapped him in the face as he pushed outside. Colt ripped at the buttons on his shirt, trying to release the noose that had apparently slipped around his throat.

He found her halfway across the resort, standing alone on the deserted beach. Moonlight streamed over her, making her look fragile. Her body curved in on itself, her arms hugging her waist. She shouldn't be sad. Not here. Not because of him. This was a place for fun and adventure. For laughter and the excitement of discovering something new.

He touched her arm, and she turned around, looking up at him with sad eyes that glistened with unshed tears. Another shock of guilt kicked through his system.

He hadn't meant to make her cry.

With a sigh, Colt gathered her into his arms and pulled her tight against him. Something deep inside him stirred at the press of her soft curves into his hard body. He ignored it.

"I'm sorry," he whispered into the crown of her hair.

Her body was stiff, her muscles tight. After several minutes, she relaxed. The emotion that had been swirling within her subsided, he could feel it slip away.

Melting into him, Lena let him take the weight of her body. His own muscles relaxed, the tension that had whipped through him easing as he realized she wouldn't hold his careless comments against him.

After several minutes she pulled away and Colt let her. She looked up at him again, calm and collected, the Lena he recognized and remembered. He was glad to see the sadness gone.

"It's not your fault," she said.

"Maybe not, but I didn't help."

Lena's lips twisted. "No, but I can't fault you for telling the truth. I knew something was wrong. Deep down, I knew. I just didn't want to admit it. Everyone was so excited. Jealous. Everyone told me how perfect Wyn was. What a wonderful husband he'd be. How lucky I was to find a great man who just happened to be heir to a fortune."

"But it didn't feel right."

Lena turned away. Reaching down, she flicked off the sandals protecting her feet. They fell to the sand with a muted plop. She walked a few steps barefoot. Colt did the same, letting his own shoes topple crookedly beside hers.

The sound of crashing waves shushed gently between them. In the distance Colt could hear the rumblings of laughter and dance music from somewhere on the island. Sometimes, like now, it was hard to remember they weren't the only people here.

"It felt right at first," she finally responded. "Wyn was sweet. We worked together for at least six months before he asked me out. I'd look up from my notes during company meetings to find him watching me instead of paying attention."

"You don't have to toe the line when daddy's in charge."

Lena reached over and shoved him. The unexpected reaction had him teetering sideways for a moment before regaining his balance.

"That isn't nice, Colt. Wyn's very good at his job."

"Yeah, so good he managed to weasel his way into a free vacation with a client."

"I was flattered."

"You were hunted, like a lion stalks an antelope. I only met the man a few times, but it was enough to realize he was charming and focused and untrustworthy."

Lena twisted, the heel of her foot grinding into the sand with the force of her motion. "Why the hell didn't you say anything?"

"Because it wasn't my place." Colt had thought about it, once, but realized he had nothing to back up his gut instinct. "I thought maybe you'd just think I was being overprotective. Playing the big-brother card or something."

A strangled sound that could have been anything from incredulity to embarrassment burst from Lena's mouth. "You're hardly my big brother."

"True. You were serious about Wyn though, and I figured he must have some qualities I couldn't see. If he'd loved you, I could have lived with it."

"But, obviously, he didn't."

The question he still had was whether she'd ever loved Wyn. Colt didn't think so, but he wasn't going to make the same mistake twice, so he wouldn't ask again.

"So, yes, in the beginning it felt right. And by the time it didn't I was in too deep. The wedding was months away and I convinced myself that it was just jitters."

Silence stretched between them. Colt had no idea what the right response was and he was afraid to say the wrong thing again.

After a few minutes Lena said, "Jeez, we're a pair. I stay in a relationship I shouldn't, and you can't stay in one more than five minutes."

"Hey, I last a hell of a lot longer than five minutes," he joked. "But I don't want to have a relationship longer than two weeks," he argued. "Too much work. Besides, I like variety in my life."

Lena grimaced. "So try a different cereal in the morning. Seriously, Colt, you need to grow up."

"When did this turn into a discussion of my short-comings?"

"I like talking about yours better than analyzing mine."

Colt laughed.

Silence stretched between them, only this time there was comfort and familiarity to it. Colt reached for her again, wrapping his arm around her shoulders and pulling her into his body. Together they stared out across the Caribbean Sea.

The jungle far behind them rustled. An animal howled in the distance. And Lena groaned quietly. "What does it say about me that I'm more upset at losing my job than my fiancé?"

"It says that you're practical," Colt said, unable to hold back a smile. Because that described Lena to a T.

"I actually think it says I'm a coward. But, dammit,

I liked my job. I was good at it and I put several hard years in at Rand Marketing."

"You are good at your job, which is why you'll be able to find something else. Graphic designers are in demand. You'll land on your feet."

"I'm pissed that I have to land at all."

"Think of it as an opportunity then. To find something better. Or maybe to work on your jewelry for a while."

He'd been upset when she'd told him she'd given up her craft. Especially because that decision had come months after she'd started dating Wyn, and Colt couldn't help but think the man was partly responsible for Lena's decision. He couldn't remember how many nights he'd watched her string together beads, bend gold wire and produce the most breathtaking and original pieces.

"You know, my sister-in-law still tells me that the earrings I gave her are the best birthday present she's ever gotten. She wears them all the time."

"I'm glad she likes them."

Colt stared up into the night sky. Stars twinkled down on them, so bright and yet too far away to touch. This conversation was beginning to feel the same way. They'd had it before, but nothing ever changed. "You're an artist, Lena, don't you long for an outlet?"

"I have an outlet. Graphic design is art."

Colt held in a snort. Maybe, but it wasn't her passion. He dropped the subject though because he knew it wouldn't get him anywhere.

"The sand's still warm." Lena looked down at her

feet, wiggling her toes in deeper. Her dark red toenails peeked out, making him want to join her in the childish gesture. Playing in the sand was something he hadn't done in a very long time. Not since his parents had died five years ago and he'd stopped joining his brother's family at the beach house.

At first, the memories had been too painful. And then it had just gotten easier to make excuses. He was out of the country. Working. Tired. Standing there with his feet pressed deep into the sand, he couldn't remember the last time he'd actually seen his brother, sister-in-law and niece. He talked to them on the phone occasionally, but he was slowly coming to realize that might not be enough.

Even the few days or weeks he'd managed to see Lena over the past couple of years had left chinks in their relationship he hadn't even been aware of. If he'd been home more, seen what was happening with Wyn, maybe he could have helped Lena avoid this mistake.

She looked over at him, a calculating expression on her face. Her eyes narrowed, and for a second he thought she was going to bring up something else he wouldn't like. Instead, she said, "Wanna race?"

He blinked, his mind trying to swiftly change gears.

Without waiting for his answer, Lena bolted for the edge of the water, leaving nothing but a spray of sand in her wake. Her happy chuckle as the waves rolled across her toes was a heck of a lot better than the sadness she'd been fighting a little while ago.

Walking slowly behind her, Colt enjoyed watching as she played in the surf. Wispy clouds passed slowly across the moon, playing peek-a-boo with the light. She twirled, her dress floating out around her body and a spray of water splashing across his face.

He thought it was an accident—until she did it again. And he couldn't let that go without retaliation. High-stepping out into the surf, Colt scooped water with both hands and threw it in her direction.

He could hear her sharp intake of breath as it rained over her. Her dress was quickly soaked, sticking to her skin. Colt had seen her body before. She'd lain out in the sun at his pool. Often enough for him to know she preferred bikinis to anything else. He'd always known she was beautiful.

But tonight, she was more than that. She was sensual and seductive without even realizing it. Her eyes sparkled. Her skin glowed. She darted in and out of the surf, taunting him, the only problem was the game he suddenly wanted to play with her had nothing to do with innocent fun.

Her foot twisted on something beneath the surface of the water. Colt watched as the expression on her face went from pleasure to panic in the space of a heartbeat. Lunging forward, he caught her, picking her up and turning toward shore.

Her arms wrapped around his neck. Her body, wet and warm, pressed against his. She looked up at him, licking stray droplets of water off her lips. His groin tightened and an answering need burst open inside him.

He growled deep in his throat, unable to stop himself. He leaned forward to claim the lips that she'd left open in invitation—intentional or not, he didn't care.

Lena's eyes went round. He felt her breath stutter against his chest. Before he could follow through, she twisted in his arms, struggling against him.

What was he doing?

Ripping his hold open, Lena dropped to the ground. The spray of her feet touching the surf landed halfway up his chest. Before he could say anything—apologize yet again—she was darting away. She didn't even stop to pick up her sandals, instead bypassing them for the fastest route back to the resort.

Some beast inside told him to run after her, to pursue her and catch her and have her right now. He ignored it, choosing instead to turn his back on the temptation. A flash of light caught Colt's attention.

Mikhail, standing several feet away, partially hidden by the jungle, stared at him with one eye. The upraised lens of his camera covered the other.

Colt's hands clenched into fists. "How long have you been there?"

"Long enough," Mikhail said, lowering his camera to let it settle heavily around his neck.

Colt wanted to make some biting retort, to expend the bubbling energy rushing through his blood. Mikhail seemed as handy a target as any.

But he didn't. Rationally, he knew the other man was simply doing his job. If the roles had been reversed, he probably would have done the same. Work was everything, and the final product held priority. He was simply not used to being on this side of the camera.

Colt had to admit that he wasn't sure he liked it. Especially if the camera—and the man wielding it—were going to be capturing things he didn't want recorded. It was one thing to pretend an attraction in front of the camera because they'd agreed to do it. It was entirely another for the camera to capture a real attraction that Colt didn't want and had no idea what to do with.

The camera didn't lie. For once, Colt wished that it would.

LENA FEIGNED SLEEP, screwing her eyes tight and burying her head into the mound of pillows when Colt returned. He'd stayed away long enough for her to rush through her nightly routine. She'd had to dig past the honeymoon negligees at the top of her suitcase for the pair of yoga pants and a tank top buried beneath. Seeing those tiny scraps of silk and lace on the heels of what had happened on the beach didn't do much for her peace of mind.

While Colt sorted quietly through his own bag, Lena fought another flash of desire. Clamping her thighs together to lessen the awakened tingle, she tried not to move beneath the covers. She had no idea what to say to Colt.

Had no idea what had really happened.

Well, obviously he'd almost kissed her. Or had she almost kissed him? She couldn't be certain. The first one, in front of Marcy, had meant nothing—for her or for him. It was playacting, and she was adult enough to go with the flow. The fact that her body had reacted was her issue to deal with. It was chemistry. Nothing more.

Now that she thought about it, she and Wyn hadn't

exactly been burning up the sheets over the past several months. Initially, she'd chalked up their lack of sex to the pressure of the wedding. They were both busy, at home and at work. Perhaps it should have been her first clue that things weren't quite right. Either way, when Colt kissed her she'd thought her dormant libido had simply chosen a bad time to rear its head.

But tonight was different. It wasn't for show. The need pulsing through her body had nothing to do with biological functions and everything to do with Colt. She'd wanted *him,* not just a male body.

It had been real. And if she wasn't mistaken, he'd felt the zing too. Which almost made it worse. How long had he wanted her? she wondered. Always? Or was this as new for him as it was for her?

What if it was simply biological for him? Romantic setting, candlelit dinner, wet clothes and close bodies.

It scared her, this unexpected reaction to Colt.

She came close to jumping in surprise when the far side of the bed dipped down with the weight of his body. She wanted to protest. The words were on her lips, although something inside her swallowed them instead of letting them out. She was supposed to be asleep.

Besides, objecting to him sleeping beside her would reveal too much. She'd have to explain why they—two grown adults, friends—couldn't share a bed without it turning sexual.

Settling on his side, his back to her, Colt let out a tiny sigh. His body rubbed against the sheets. The rasping sound suddenly seemed very intimate.

Lena lay there, listening to the steady rise and fall of his breathing. She felt her own lungs synchronize with his. The sheets that had minutes before seemed cool and comforting were suddenly smothering, cocooning them together. She wanted to fling them off, but couldn't. His heat melted into her. Her body twitched, fighting to snuggle closer.

Colt dropped off within minutes. She envied him that ability to sleep wherever. She also resented that he wasn't fighting the same urges that kept her tossing and turning.

She was going to look awesome in the morning. She knew the camera added ten pounds. She wondered what it did with bags beneath the eyes.

Several times during the night Lena awoke to find her body curled tightly against Colt's. Once her leg had been thrown across his thighs. She'd quickly rolled back onto her side of the bed only to wake again with her derriere snuggled into the cradle of his thighs and his hand cupped possessively around her breast.

As if the physical contact wasn't bad enough, the dreams that had interrupted her sleep in the first place were almost worse—filled with frustrating shadows and tempting heat. Her mind certainly had no problems conjuring up exotic and tantalizing ways Colt could pleasure her.

Even now, close to dawn, her body hummed with a level of sexual frustration she hadn't felt since her teenage years. She didn't like it. It made her feel out of control, possessed by her own desire.

She would not let it rule her. Especially with Colt.

They had too much history to throw everything away on a fling. He was important to her, which also made the whole thing more complicated. She already loved him. Add sex and there was the strong possibility she would fall in love with him.

And that would be terrible. Their friendship worked because they didn't have expectations. Colt called when he called. He came into town when it was convenient. He was a nomad and liked it that way.

She just couldn't live like that. The thought alone made her want to break out in hives. She'd moved enough in her life and didn't want to do it again. In fact, she'd been dreading moving from her apartment into Wyn's. She'd put it off until the last possible second. Her apartment had been the first home she'd ever had. She'd bought it with her own hard-earned money and could admit she'd been reluctant to give up that sanctuary.

No, bottom line was that she and Colt would make a terrible couple. They might enjoy a few days rolling through a sexual fog, but when it cleared they'd both realize it was a mistake.

They hadn't done anything that couldn't be forgotten. Better to stop things now before they went further.

5

LENA WAS GONE when Colt woke up. Just as well, since he was sporting a rather obvious erection and probably would have done something stupid—like capture her mouth again—if he'd woken up next to her. However, when she hadn't returned a little while later, he began to worry.

As if on cue, some animal let out a screech from the jungle.

Several frantic minutes of searching led him to a thatched hut down the beach. If he hadn't seen her red-tipped toes peeking out of the structure he probably would have missed her.

"There you are. I've been looking for you everywhere," he said, his words sounding slightly accusatory even to his own ears. He tried to soften them with a bright smile. Something in his chest twisted for a moment before letting go, releasing a tension he hadn't been aware of until it was gone.

Her eyes were slightly unfocused when she looked up at him. He might have wondered if she'd already started in on the fruity drinks, but as he watched, her eyes cleared. She looked around, slowly taking in her surroundings as if seeing them for the first time.

"What time is it?"

"Almost nine. I expect Marcy will be hunting us down soon."

Lena shrugged. "I hope she has something fun planned."

Colt crouched in front of her, his feet digging into the sand. He noticed she had a pile of shells and smooth stones in front of her. Some were whole. Some were broken. But all held a sort of wild beauty that came only from nature.

She'd arranged several—handpicked he'd bet—into a descending swirl that echoed the pattern of the shells themselves. The subtle shift of color gave the piece a feel of inherent movement, like sunlight filtered through water.

"That's beautiful."

Her hand fell on top, crushing the middle shells deeper into the sand and marring the perfection. "It's nothing. My version of doodling."

Colt frowned, but didn't argue. Lena pushed up from the ground, forcing him to move back if he didn't want to get knocked over. She ran her hands across the seat of her shorts, cleaning off the sand. Some stubborn grains clung to her legs. Colt thought about reaching down and brushing them away but caught himself just in time. The last thing he needed was to feel her smooth skin beneath his fingers, not if he expected to get through the day without embarrassing himself.

"I'm hungry. Any idea where we could get breakfast?"

They were rounding the curve of the beach heading back to the civilization of the resort when Marcy appeared before them. Her steps were quick and purposeful. Mikhail trailed behind her at a more sedate pace.

"There you are. We need to get started."

Lena's stomach growled and she and Colt glanced at each other, sharing a smile. The awkwardness that had settled over them disappeared. Colt let out a sigh of relief, feeling back on solid ground for the first time since he'd kissed her.

They walked around the resort, posing for photographs at various spots along the way. It was easy, comfortable, to wander around, laughing, touching, teasing each other. After a few hours—and a quick stop at the breakfast buffet—they ended up at the pool.

The midafternoon heat had set in and they were both starting to wilt. Changing into the bathing suits Marcy provided them was a welcome relief.

Mikhail set a scene with towel-draped lounge chairs, sweating glasses of some tropical drink and abandoned books sitting open at the foot of their chairs. For the next thirty minutes they worked, moving where Mikhail told them, smiling on cue, the temptation of the pool just a few feet away almost cruel.

A crowd of people gathered around them, not overtly gawking, but definitely watching as Mikhail put Colt and Lena through their paces.

"I think I'm melting," Lena mumbled through a smile that was looking more fake by the second.

Her skin was flushed, glistening beneath the sun. His eyes raked down her body. He couldn't help it. The turquoise bikini she'd put on revealed more of her than he'd seen in a very long time. Her flat stomach, pert little breasts, long legs…

Colt swallowed. A hard need twisted through him and his body stirred. Lena's eyes sharpened. Her lips parted. She leaned closer to him and suddenly the heat was absolutely oppressive.

"That's great, guys. We're done. Marcy needs you later, but for now you can enjoy the pool." Mikhail dismissed them, turning to his equipment and leaving Colt floundering once again.

He did not like the sensation. Never in his entire life had he been this out of his element with a woman. Hell, he was known for his love affairs. They were short, intense and satisfying for all parties involved. Easy.

Nothing about Lena was easy. If she'd been anyone else, he would have seduced her last night and been done with it. It wouldn't be the first vacation fling he'd ever had.

But it was Lena. And she deserved so much more than a fling.

She wanted permanent. The white picket fence, kids and a dog. And he knew that wasn't something he could give her…even if he'd been inclined to try.

Sex was not supposed to be this complicated.

He was just about to suggest they both jump into the water—if for no other reason than it would cover up the temptation of her body—when a woman popped up at the end of their chairs.

"Y'all are the honeymooning couple they're taking photographs of, aren't you?" The perky little blonde had a wide smile and friendly eyes.

Lena looked across at him as if to say *save me*.

"Uh, yeah, they're photographing us."

Without an invitation, the blonde plopped her rear onto the end of Lena's chair.

"I thought so. I think y'all have the bungalow next to ours. I saw y'all come in yesterday." The girl leaned closer to Lena, mock-whispering as if they'd been friends forever, "We're honeymooning, too. I'm so glad the wedding hoopla is finally over. I wanted to elope, but Daddy insisted on throwing a big party." She sighed, rolling her eyes. "The things we do for our parents, right?" An indulgent smile belied the martyr act she was playing.

Lena stared at the other woman. Colt's lips twitched with humor at seeing her speechless. The chatty interloper didn't seem to notice Lena's lack of participation in the conversation, she just breezed right on.

"Where are my manners?" She giggled, sticking out her hand, first to Lena and then to him. "I'm Georgia Ann but everyone just calls me Georgie."

"Quit bothering these nice people, Georgie." A man walked up, dark-haired, young, an apologetic expression on his face. But the minute his eyes landed on his wife, that expression disappeared, replaced by a sort of adoration that Colt found fascinating. "Georgie's never met a stranger in her life."

"Guilty as charged." She smiled. Colt realized that Lena was now smiling, too. There was something about the woman's friendly, infectious attitude that was too hard to resist. Like a tractor beam, she pulled you in. "This is Wesley, love of my life." She stared up into his face, her eyes twinkling with a brightness that hadn't been there moments before.

They might have been sickening, if the love they shared hadn't been so obviously genuine.

Lena looked across at him, her eyes wide. Colt shrugged. They'd leave eventually.

Wesley's hand dropped onto Georgie's shoulder. She leaned back against him. "We're thinking about hiking into the jungle tomorrow. We hear there's a beautiful waterfall. What are y'all doing?" Without waiting for their answer, she bounced against the chair, looked up at Wesley and said, "I have an excellent idea."

"Uh-oh" was his response, despite the fact that a smile stretched across his face.

Turning back to them, she grabbed Lena's hand. "Why don't y'all come with us? It'll be fun. We can bring a picnic, bond over horror stories of the wedding. My aunt Millie gave us the ugliest lamp you've ever seen. I think she pulled it out of her attic. I swear the thing has got to be fifty years old if it's a day. It'll probably catch our house on fire."

Lena shot Colt a panicked look. "I think we have—" she started.

Wesley shot him a knowing expression. "Take my advice and just say yes now. It'll be less painful that way."

Georgie piped up, "I won't take no. Leave everything to me." Scooting up from her chair, she began to walk away, still talking. "We'll meet you outside your bungalow at ten sharp. I'll pack the picnic."

The excuse Colt was going to use lay useless on his tongue as the couple rounded the other side of the pool.

"What just happened?" Lena asked, flopping back into her chair.

"I think we're going on a picnic in the jungle tomorrow."

Lena blinked. "What if Marcy needs us?"

"I suppose she'll just have to get over it. Or maybe she could get us out of the picnic."

Lena looked across the pool to where Georgie and Wesley had settled back into their own lounge chairs. Georgie waved. Lena lifted her hand in a half-hearted response.

"I don't think even Marcy could stop her. I'm exhausted just listening to her."

"Hey, on the bright side, we get to see the waterfall."

"And on the dark side, they think we're married."

"I thought that was what you wanted."

"Sure, but I didn't think we'd be spending time with anyone but Marcy and Mikhail who already know. I figured if we talked to anyone it would only be for a few minutes and then it would be over."

Colt looked across at Georgie and Wesley and felt a grimace turn his lips. They were so happy and in love they would surely pick up on the fact that he and Lena weren't. "We could always explain."

"Horror of horrors. I can just hear Georgie's gushing sympathy right now." She looked over at him, a pained expression on her face. "I don't think I could take that.

It was bad enough dealing with the chaos at the wedding."

"Then I guess if we can't get out of it we'll be married. That doesn't sound so bad, does it?"

Her eyes sharpened with a deep intensity that he didn't quite understand. Slowly, she answered, "I suppose not."

LENA HAD NO IDEA what they were doing. All they'd been told was to disappear for a while and to return to their bungalow at eight sharp. Obviously, Marcy's next photo shoot had something to do with their room. Fine.

In the meantime, she and Colt had finally managed to get into the pool. The water had been heavenly. They'd skipped the dining room in favor of fattening fried foods at the snack shack. The atmosphere was completely different, which was a good thing. The last thing she needed was another romantic meal with Colt. Playing around in the pool had been bad enough.

Grabbing his ankles to dunk him in. Her fingers grazing across the tight wall of his abs. His body sliding against her beneath the water. Lena gulped, squeezing her eyes shut and hoping the building storm of awareness would disappear, like the monster that couldn't hurt her if she couldn't see it.

The problem was it was still there, eyes open or closed.

The more time they spent together, the more aware of him she became. Lena was beginning to worry that ignoring her stirring emotions wasn't going to be enough. They were getting more powerful, more demanding.

She needed to get hold of herself and her libido. The problem was she no longer trusted that she could actually control either one. And she was starting to question why she needed to—why couldn't she have him?

A shiver raced down her spine as she remembered the exquisite pleasure of his body rubbing against hers.

"Are you cold?" Colt asked from behind, his palm landing gently at the small of her back.

Ripples of awareness continued through her body like rings from a stone hitting a pond. She wanted him to go on touching her forever, which was why she shook off his hold and said, "No, I'm fine," tossing a smile over her shoulder to take the sting of her rebuke away.

They rounded the corner in the path to see Marcy waiting for them, the door to their bungalow standing wide open behind her.

Marcy swept them inside and with a grand gesture of her arm, indicated the single room.

It had been completely changed.

The couch and end tables had been removed, along with the small table and chairs in the eating nook. The beautifully carved wooden bed had been placed in the center of the room, and draped with gauzy white material that fluttered on an easy breeze. Someone—probably Marcy—had flung open every door and window, letting in the scent of tropical flowers and the salty tang of the sea.

Drippy, mismatched candles had been placed across

the few remaining surfaces—a faux mantel, the kitchen counter and even the floor.

There was no question, this was a seduction scene taken directly from the most romantic and unforgettable movie she'd ever wanted to see. And Marcy clearly expected her to star in it. With Colt. Lena swallowed and waves of heat washed across her skin. Anticipation mixed with dread. Her worst nightmare and hottest dream all mixed into one.

Colt spun slowly in the center of the room. "Someone's been busy," he drawled, leaving to interpretation whether his words were complimentary or derogatory.

Lena narrowed her eyes, studying his face, trying to figure out what he thought about all of this. Was he horrified? Or, possibly, intrigued?

"We aim to please," said Marcy, grasping Lena by the elbow and pulling her along behind her. "I have several outfits for you to choose from. Whatever you're most comfortable in is fine with me."

"What kind of outfits?" Colt asked, his voice going dark.

"Nothing like that," Marcy admonished. "We're not going for salacious here. We want a few romantic shots highlighting the private bungalows that are available to our couples."

Marcy pushed Lena into the bathroom, closing the door behind her. The wood creaked as she leaned against it. With trepidation, Lena took in the row of soft, filmy fabrics Marcy had lined up for her. She had to admit that considering where they were filming, the choices could have been worse. Not a bustier or padded bra in the mix.

Lena reached for one, a pale pink color that probably wouldn't look great with her fair skin. But it was so soft beneath her fingers. She reached for another, this one dark red. Lena was afraid it would make her look as though she was trying too hard. She liked the black gown with lace edging, but it just seemed too stark somehow.

The final one had drawn her eye immediately which was why she'd saved it for last. To say that it was blue was somehow wrong. It was, but it had an iridescent shine to it that captured every shifting shade from the water outside their door. It was light and dark and bright and soft all at once.

It was perfect.

Slipping it on over her head, Lena felt as if she were wearing water instead of silk. It was longer than she'd expected, skimming just above the curve of her knee. The spaghetti straps might have left her feeling exposed, but the neckline was cut high enough to cover her cleavage so that helped. As far as lingerie went, it was enticing but not revealing.

Lena looked at herself in the mirror and felt a flutter of nerves, anticipation and hope deep in her stomach. She was…sexy. It wasn't that she'd never thought of herself that way. She had. Just not with Colt waiting in the other room. Taking a deep breath, she headed out.

The sun had begun to sink as they'd come into the bungalow. Now it was almost completely down, just the rim of gray, gold and pink at the edge of the world brushing the room with a soft, romantic glow.

Colt's eyes were bright as they slowly perused her body, taking in every inch of her. Her skin tingled and tightened. Lena shifted, trying to find some way to relieve the pressure that was mounting inside her.

His intensity was unnerving. She'd never seen this side of him. Lena wanted to back away, to pretend that none of this was happening. Instead, she found her feet moving slowly toward him, as if drawn by a gravitational pull she couldn't see, but definitely felt.

Thank God Marcy broke the spell by clearing her throat. Embarrassment at forgetting they weren't alone flamed up Lena's face and body.

"Mikhail, what do you think?"

The photographer joined them in the middle of the room. He looked over at Lena for several seconds. "Lena, what do you think of being on the bed, with Colt in the background?" The other man was warming to the vision only he could see.

"With her almost blurry and slightly romantic?" Colt asked.

And apparently Colt saw the same thing. Gone was the devouring expression from moments before, replaced by a studied gaze as he contemplated what the lens would see. It had been a very long time since Lena had watched him work.

During college, his camera had been like an extension of his hand, always present and subject to being pulled out at a moment's notice. Walks around the city had turned into photojournalism sessions. Heck, on occasion that lens had even turned on her. She wondered if he'd kept any of the photographs of her from years ago.

"Exactly." The two men walked off for several paces, their heads bent together as they talked about shutter speed, light and exposure—things Lena didn't fully understand. With nothing better to do, she climbed up onto the mattress.

She felt like a fool, stretched out across the cream silk sheets, which were not the standard Escape issue. Considering the price this bungalow rented for, they should be.

"So, what's the story?" Marcy leaned against one of the posts at the foot of the bed, her eyes friendly and curious.

"What do you mean?"

Lena shifted, using the pretense of arranging her legs and the silk gown to avoid looking into Marcy's eyes.

"There's more going on with you two than meets the eye."

"I told you, we're old friends."

"Please. I've spent the last two years managing a resort that specializes in selling sex—tasteful and romantic sex but sex nonetheless. I know chemistry when I see it. He couldn't keep his eyes off you when you walked out here. And the minute you stepped through that door he was the first thing you wanted to see."

Lena's eyes were drawn across the room to Colt. She couldn't help herself even though it was a dead give-away.

"It's…complicated."

"Isn't everything?" Marcy asked. "He is beautiful," she added, her eyes cataloguing Colt in a purely academic way.

Lena was used to women staring at Colt, calculating whether he was available and if she was competition. There was absolutely no interest in Marcy's gaze.

"Athletic, with enough little-boy charm and mischief to make him approachable," Marcy analyzed. She leveled a pointed look at Lena.

"He moves around a lot. No roots. Anything we start would be short-lived and when it was over our friendship would never be the same."

"That's assuming it ends."

"It would. Colt doesn't form attachments."

"Except to you."

"I told you, we're just friends," Lena protested.

"Isn't friendship an attachment?"

"It isn't the same."

"But it's something. More than he's had with anyone else, I'd hazard. It's easy to dump someone you don't really like, harder to walk away from someone who's already important."

For no good reason fear swamped Lena. Her mouth felt dry and gritty, as if she'd swallowed sand. A bone-deep chill washed over her and her hands began to tremble.

That was exactly what she was afraid of. If she gave in to this and he walked away, could she survive? For the first time in her life, she understood how her mother had found herself repeatedly ruled by her emotions. They were too overwhelming to ignore.

Even though she knew giving in would be a mistake.

"Everyone ready?" Mikhail asked, interrupting Lena's little panic attack. She wanted desperately to say no, to rush out of the room, away from Colt, from temptation, from inevitable heartache. But she didn't. She couldn't. Not with Colt standing in front of her, a concerned expression on his face.

"Are you okay?"

She swallowed, the lump of sand in her throat refusing to budge. He moved closer, reaching for her. Lena scooted away, knowing if he touched her right now she would erupt into an inferno of demanding need neither of them could control.

Unable to speak, she nodded. And hoped it was enough.

6

"LENA, CAN YOU LOOK a little more longingly at Colt? Extend your lines. You're yearning for him. Trying to get him to come to you, to join you."

Mikhail had been barking orders at Lena for the last twenty minutes, clearly not enamored with her performance. Colt had no idea what was going on with her. She'd gone from relaxed and enjoying the process this afternoon to uneasy and awkward. Maybe the gown was making her uncomfortable, although she hadn't appeared so when she'd walked out in it. She'd looked sexy, confident in her allure as a woman. Besides, the bikini she'd worn earlier had covered far less.

Colt bit down on the inside of his cheek to keep from snapping at Mikhail. He realized the photographer was just trying to get the picture he needed. But the more he barked at Lena the stiffer she became. She wasn't a natural model. She was beautiful, poised and self-contained, not an exhibitionist who relished displaying herself and her emotions for the world to view.

"This isn't working." Mikhail dropped his camera to his side with a huff of frustration.

"If you'd stop growling at her then maybe you'd get what you want." So much for trying not to interject and make things worse.

"Do you have a better idea?"

As a matter of fact, he did. "Can we clear everyone else out?"

Marcy began to sputter in protest, but one look from Mikhail seemed to stop her in her tracks.

"Sure." It took exactly five minutes for Mikhail's assistants and Marcy to clear the room. By the time they were gone the sun had completely sunk and the lighting was actually better—darkness outside and romantic, flickering lights inside. Mikhail took the opportunity to fiddle with the light stands in the corners, adjusting for the changes.

Lena flopped back against the jewel-toned pillows piled high at the headboard, her arm flung across her face. "When will the torture end?"

"Torture?" Colt asked, walking around the headboard to stand above her. The gown covering her shimmered in the shifting light, making it look as if her body undulated beneath the thin layer of silk. A sharp spike of need lanced through him. His fingers curled into his palms to keep from reaching for her.

But he couldn't stop himself from moving closer. Placing a knee on the bed beside her, he enjoyed the way she rolled toward him, her hip bumping against the inside of his thigh.

Even as he bent above her, words he hadn't meant to

say fell from his lips. "The only torture has been watching you writhe around on this bed and not being able to touch you." His words were guttural, primal, pulled from a place deep inside him that he didn't want to acknowledge but couldn't seem to contain.

She gasped, her eyes widening as she looked up at him. He watched her swallow, the long column of her throat working.

"Then touch me," she whispered, the words pulled from her body as reluctantly as his had been. He heard the hesitation, understood it.

But couldn't seem to do the right thing.

Her features were taut. Her eyes glittered, possessed by the same driving need that pulsed inside him. It was new, startling, tempting.

Colt slowly reached for her, running a single finger down the exposed curve of her arm. Her skin was so soft.

Her breath hitched. He heard the sound, saw the catch as her chest rose, paused and finished the climb.

In the back of his brain Colt heard the click of the camera, but this time he didn't let it matter. Nothing could distract him from Lena.

Her lips parted in anticipation. His finger continued over the slippery silk that covered her body. He brushed the side of her breast and watched in fascination as the nipple, so close he could have reached out and touched it, puckered and jutted towards him.

He stopped at the curve of her hip, pressing his curled fingers into the mattress for balance. He loomed over her, expecting that at any moment she'd come to her senses and tell him to stop.

But she didn't.

Instead, she arched beneath him, exposing the long, slim line of her neck. Her hair, darker in the low light, fanned out around her. He wanted to bury his fingers in the thick mass, use it to hold her to him.

The gown she was wearing pulled tight across her chest. He was sure there was some name for the neckline, probably something tantalizing and provocative since it tempted him with the curve of her flesh beneath the slick material. He didn't know what it was though, and frankly didn't care.

Her eyelids drooped heavily over mesmerizing blue-gray eyes. She was a temptress, pulling him in and making him forget why he shouldn't have her.

His lips drifted across her skin. He licked at the pulse point pounding against her throat. He breathed her in, consuming the scent of her as it swirled around them both. Dark, mysterious, feminine.

He latched on to her skin and sucked, drawing a sigh of pleasure from her as she surrendered to whatever he wanted.

What he wanted was her.

With an answering growl, Colt dove in and claimed her lips. She opened for him as he pushed inside. This kiss was completely different from the one they'd shared before. It wasn't soft and persuasive. It was fire and heat and devouring desire. It was demanding and yearning and the release of denying what he wanted.

In the back of his mind red warning lights were

flashing, but he was too far gone to care. His hands were rough as they pulled her to him. His fingers tore at the silk covering her body. He needed to feel her. Touch her. Own her.

Make her his…

The loud slam of the door had him shooting up and off the bed.

But she wasn't his.

Lena looked up at him, a mixture of embarrassment, horror and desire swamping her eyes. Her chest, now barely covered by the slip of soft fabric, rose and fell in halting time to his own uneven heartbeat.

He'd almost made a huge mistake. He liked things casual. He never slept with anyone he truly cared for, which made it easy to walk away.

He couldn't walk away from Lena. Once Pandora's box was opened there would be no going back.

And that scared the shit out of him.

Backing slowly toward the door, Colt couldn't pull his gaze from Lena's. Not even as he fumbled behind him for the knob and slipped out into the comforting darkness.

A KNOCK ON THE DOOR HAD LENA bolting up in the bed. Her hair hung limply into her bleary eyes. She pushed the mop away, clearing her vision, and then regretted it when the bright morning sunshine speared straight into her brain. Squinting, she mumbled a curse and stumbled for the entrance to the bungalow.

To anyone else it probably appeared as if she'd been on a five-day bender. The reality was that she'd gotten barely a few hours' sleep, and those had come in random snatches between crazy nightmares and erotic dreams—both featuring Colt.

She had no idea where he was, but he definitely hadn't shared the bed with her last night. If he was the one on the other side of the door it was entirely possible she might kill him.

Somewhere during the night she'd gone from relief that he'd had the forethought to stop what they'd started, to anger that he'd walked out without a word, to worry that he'd do something stupid such as hike into the jungle in the middle of the night and fall off a cliff.

The pounding increased, joined by the cheerful sound of Georgie's drawl. "Wake up, sleepyheads. We've been waiting on y'all for a half hour."

Lena's right eye began to twitch, but she opened the door anyway.

Georgie leveled a knowing, conspiratorial look in her direction as she brushed past into their bungalow. "Someone had a fun night."

Lena self-consciously patted her hair, trying in vain to smooth out the knots.

"Honey, you look like you've been rode hard and put up wet. At least tell me the ride was worth it." Georgie took in their bungalow. "Well, this is…interesting. A little different layout than ours." The frown on her face said she wasn't impressed.

"Marcy moved everything around. We had a photo session last night." Lena couldn't stop the hot flush that burned her skin at the memories. A stinging heat settled between her thighs and she shifted from one foot to the other, trying to find relief.

"Where's Colt?" Georgie asked, her puzzled eyes looking around the space as if he might pop out from beneath the kitchen sink.

Lena opened her mouth to tell a lie—although she wasn't sure which one—but the dark rumble of Colt's voice stopped her.

"Right here," he said, leaning against the open doorway out to the patio and private pool. Had he been out there the whole time?

Arms crossed over his chest, he lounged there, looking for all the world like a relaxed—sated—groom. His wide chest was naked, a tempting V of hair running in an arrow down his body to disappear beneath the lowriding band of his jeans.

Lena swallowed, her mouth suddenly dry and useless. Colt's eyes flashed for a moment as they ran over her body, rekindling what he hadn't been willing to finish last night.

Lena's hands crumpled into fists at her side, although she wasn't sure who she wanted to use them on more—Colt or her unruly libido.

Georgie reached out to pat her arm, grinning slyly. "Don't worry, sweetheart. Looks like someone has enough stamina for both of you."

Colt's lips twitched. Lena's eyes narrowed in warning. Clearing his throat, he said, "Why don't you give us time to get ready, Georgie? We're obviously running a little late."

"Twenty minutes," she said, swinging a perfectly

manicured nail to point at both of them. "Or we're leaving without you."

"Promise?" Lena muttered beneath her breath. It was Colt's turn to flash *her* a warning glance, ushering Georgie out with promises that they'd be there.

Not waiting for him to return, Lena went into the bathroom and rummaged through her toiletry bag until she found some aspirin. Thanks to her restless night, her brain felt as if it was trying to push straight through the top of her skull. Not bothering with water, she swallowed the tablets dry and then regretted it when Colt asked, "Everything all right," and the chalky lump stopped somewhere in the middle of her throat.

Pushing past him, she made a beeline for the fridge and the Diet Coke Marcy had stocked there. Popping the top, she swallowed several gulps.

"Slow down," he said, propping his hip against the counter, pulling the edge of his worn jeans down far enough that she could see the jutting tip of his hip. She gulped some more, tearing her eyes away from his body.

"Caffeine. I have a headache."

Colt frowned. "Maybe we shouldn't go."

A few minutes earlier, Lena would have jumped at the chance to back out of spending hours on end with little miss sunshine. But as her eyes strayed to the bed still sitting in the middle of the room, she realized there were worse ideas in the world.

Like being alone with Colt. With chaperones she was less likely to throw herself at him like a wanton hussy.

Besides, the alternative was whatever Marcy had

scheduled for the day, and frankly, after last night she was afraid to find out what that might entail.

Pretending for the camera had gotten seriously complicated. She no longer knew what was fake and what was real. Where her friendship with Colt ended and her attraction began.

Part of her was grateful Colt had put a stop to things last night. But most of her was just frustrated.

Yeah, putting people between them was probably the intelligent choice.

She reluctantly said, "No, I want to go. Wild jungle, tropical waterfall, sounds like a great way to spend the day." Unfortunately, her tingling body reminded her there were plenty of more enjoyable ways to pass the time.

TREKKING THROUGH THE JUNGLE was not exactly what he'd had in mind. Although, after last night, what he had in mind was out of the question. It had taken everything inside him not to grab Lena and throw her down on the looming bed this morning.

Getting out of the bungalow and away from temptation had seemed like the best plan.

Ahead, Georgie and Wesley walked hand in hand through the jungle. The path was barely wide enough to accommodate them, probably meant for single file hiking. But that didn't deter them. Colt noticed they were always touching. Nothing major, the brush of his hand across her back or her arm around his waist.

His palms itched to reach for Lena, to pull her next to him just to know that she was there. Instead, he let her walk a few steps in front. The hem of the tiny shorts she'd put on barely covered the bottom swell of her ass. Colt couldn't pull his gaze away, constantly hoping for a bigger glimpse.

It was making the whole situation more difficult. Hiking he could handle. Hiking with a raging hard-on was far from enjoyable. Although, he had to admit the view was damn nice and more than worth the discomfort.

Without even looking behind her, Lena said, "Stop staring at my ass."

Colt probably should have felt guilty for being caught. He didn't.

"How'd you know I was looking?"

She peered over her shoulder, raking him with a laser gaze. "Because I can feel it."

His entire body tightened. His veins pulsed, too small to contain the quick shot of desire.

"You're the one who walked away, Colt. Don't get me wrong, I'm glad. It would have been a mistake. But you can't leave like that and then stare at my ass like it's the first bite of the best meal of your life."

She shot him another glance, this one a little darker with promise. "It isn't fair."

What wasn't fair was having her prance around in tempting clothes without expecting a reaction.

"I'm a man, Lena. What do you want from me?"

She stopped on the path, spinning to face him. "I don't know anymore," she said, the harsh words carrying an air of reluctant honesty.

Colt stepped into her space, toe-to-toe. He towered

over her. He had to admire the way she tipped her head back and stared straight into his eyes, defiant and determined to stand her ground and not let him—or their situation—intimidate her.

Deep in her eyes he saw the same emotions he was fighting against. Confusion. Awareness. Fear, hope, heat.

They were in over their heads, but he realized at least they'd drown together. Maybe there was a way for this to work, for them to release the energy building between them, without ruining what they already had.

There was a term for it, right? Friends with benefits. He'd never understood the appeal until now.

"Admit it. You wore those shorts on purpose."

Her eyes widened and she gave a little shake of her head, the motion sending her bangs into her eyes. With a gentle brush of his fingers, he pushed the hair back so that he could see her expression. Her eyes flared at the simple connection, her pupils contracting.

He could tell she wanted to look away. But, just like him, she was caught in the moment and couldn't let go. "Maybe."

His thumb stroked down the line of her cheek to her jaw. Her lips parted, giving him an unobstructed view of her little pink tongue. He wanted to reach inside and stroke it with his own.

And he might have, if they hadn't been reminded they had company by Georgie's amazed exclamation. "It's so beautiful!"

In that moment he heard the shushed roar and wondered if it had been there the whole time.

"Hurry up, y'all." Georgie's voice floated down the path.

Lena had already turned to follow. Colt rushed to catch up with her. This time when the urge to run his hand along her spine hit, he didn't tamp it down. Instead, he reached for her and relished the way her muscles jumped and her body pressed into his touch.

They broke through the trees a few minutes later. The waterfall was beautiful, with an untouched quality that Colt knew couldn't be real. There was a path cut straight to it after all. They weren't the first humans to visit here. Heck, probably not even the first this week.

"Look at this place. It's gorgeous," Lena breathed.

Colt walked into the clearing that surrounded the pool where the water from the falls collected before it broke through the rest of the jungle in a quiet line. He was struck by how calm the water was, especially considering that it was tumbling over a cliff twenty feet above them to churn over large boulders and rocks just a few feet away.

How could something so violent turn so calm within such a space? Mother Nature truly deserved respect for her awe-inspiring beauty.

Lena walked up beside him. Her arm brushed against his and a shock shot through his body, stronger than anything he'd ever experienced before.

"Look at those colors. What I wouldn't give to be able to capture them in a stone or a shell or a piece of glass." Colt heard the same awe in her voice that was expanding his chest.

"Why don't you?"

"Because I can't. No stone or glass could produce

something so pure and vibrant. There are just some things that can't be replicated and I refuse to create a cheap imitation."

Her integrity was impressive, but something he'd always known she possessed. She expected a lot from herself and the people around her. Which made it worse when those people failed her as her mother and Wyn had.

Colt had the sudden urge to protect her, to make sure nothing ever hurt her again. But he, more than anyone, realized that wasn't possible. No one could stop the inevitable.

All you could do was minimize your exposure and protect yourself as best you could.

"Soups on, y'all," Georgie called out. She'd been busy spreading a blanket beneath the soaring trees. An array of food sat in sealed containers. She'd even brought real silverware and plastic plates.

Colt shot Wesley a commiserating look. The poor bastard had packed it all into the jungle. Wesley shrugged. "My baby prides herself on hospitality."

"I do know how to throw a party, don't I?" she asked, with a proud smile.

The four of them settled onto opposite corners of the blanket. Wesley speared a bite of broccoli salad off of Georgie's plate. She swatted at his hand, but followed the empty gesture by offering what was already on her fork.

They all seemed to settle into a comfortable companionship. Lena managed to steer Georgie away from the topic of their wedding whenever the other woman wanted to hear details, although he did catch her fiddling with the gold band around her finger several times. They talked about their lives, it turned out Georgie was a counselor at an elementary school and Wesley had just taken over running his family's car dealership.

They were fascinated by all the places Colt's job had taken him.

"That'll be so much fun for a while. Moving around, seeing new places, experiencing new things." Georgie looked up at Wesley with a sad smile on her face. "I envy y'all that flexibility. Wesley's a bit tied down."

"I told you I'd quit tomorrow if that's what you want me to do."

"I don't." She patted his leg, leaning into his body. "I'd rather have boring and ordinary with you than exotic without you."

Lena made an incredulous sound that she quickly turned into a cough.

"Let's cool off," Wesley suggested. They all made quick work of cleaning up. The water was cool and refreshing, washing away the heat of the hike. Even as he tried to behave himself, Colt found his hands and mind straying to Lena.

Despite the friendly atmosphere, a pulsing undercurrent ran between them every time their gazes caught and held. It was torture, having her so close and knowing he couldn't do anything about it.

7

SOMEWHERE IN THE LATE afternoon the four of them drowsed beneath the sun. Filtered through the canopy of the trees above, the light was washed out and soft against their skin.

Lena pretended to settle, although she was too restless to actually get comfortable.

Between last night and this morning something had changed. She could see it in Colt's eyes, the way he watched her. He no longer tried to cover up the interest she could now see clearly. Instead, he tortured her with it, letting his eyes roam across her body the way she wanted his hands to touch her.

In the water, he'd teased her, letting his hand brush across her sensitive breasts before pulling away. His fingers had slid up the smooth expanse of her thigh only to disappear before giving her what she wanted.

She'd tried to play the same game, but he was too fast.

Beside her, Colt shifted. Pushing soundlessly to his feet, he walked several paces away, paused long enough to scoop up the pack he'd brought, looked over his shoulder at her, and then continued past the water to disappear into the cool shadows of the jungle.

She had a decision to make. She could follow him, finish what had been building between them. Or she could stay on the blanket, yearning twisting her insides into knots, and walk back to the resort frustrated and disappointed.

The second option held absolutely no appeal.

As Lena pushed to her feet, Georgie raised her head and looked over.

"Don't wait for us," Lena whispered.

Georgie gave her a drowsy, knowing smile but didn't say anything. Instead, she laid her head back onto Wesley's shoulder, snuggling deep into his arms.

On silent feet, Lena followed Colt into the jungle. She softly whispered his name, but he didn't reply. She moved farther, letting the gigantic trees and thick underbrush swallow her. Not even the rush of the waterfall could penetrate the dense growth around her.

She was about to turn back, certain she must have gone in a different direction from Colt, when his hands wrapped around her waist.

She let out a surprised squeak which Colt's devouring mouth immediately swallowed.

Surprise mixed with adrenaline, but even as her mind raced to catch up her body was already melting into him. His arms wrapped around her, lifting her up onto her toes and crushing her against him. Their tongues warred, sucked, played. His hands wandered. It would have been so easy to just let the moment take her and deal with the consequences later. But that wasn't who she was.

Pulling away from him, Lena drew in a deep breath. Colt didn't take the hint, instead latching his mouth onto the sensitive side of her neck. Her knees buckled and he caught her, scooping her into his arms.

Carrying her a few feet, Colt laid her onto the silvery surface of an emergency blanket. It crinkled loudly beneath her body.

"Where did this come from?" she asked.

"I was a Boy Scout. 'Always be prepared.' This pack has been all over the world with me and it's always ready."

He dropped to his knees beside her, adding his own rustling to the muted sounds of the jungle around them. In this moment, it was easy to believe they were the only people in the entire world.

He leaned over her, ready to pick up where they'd left off, but Lena stopped him, pushing her hand between them. Her fingers connected with his lips and even that shot a tiny spark through her blood. But this was important.

"What changed?" she asked, hoping with every fiber of her being that she liked his answer.

He drew back from her, rocking onto his heels. "I don't know."

That wasn't what she wanted to hear. Pulling her legs beneath her, she was ready to get up and walk away, but he stopped her.

"I'm tired of fighting it, Lena. I've wanted you for days. Probably longer, if I was honest with myself. It was easy to ignore when we were continents away. I'd come home, feel a little buzz when we were together, and leave again. I'd convince myself it wasn't real. Or I'd stay away long enough to forget it."

"I was so easy to forget?"

He bent down, pressing his forehead to hers, whispering, "No. But I don't want to change what we've already got." He pulled back, looking into her eyes. A shadow of something clouded the bright green surface.

"I think it's too late for that. The minute we stepped onto this island it was inevitable."

"I can't promise you anything."

She swallowed, recognizing exactly what he was telling her. Nothing that she didn't already know. They had two completely different lives that only intersected on occasion. He was the worst possible man for her, but apparently that didn't mean anything to her wayward body.

"I don't remember asking you for a promise. What I want is for you to make me feel. To make me forget. To give me everything you've got for however long we have. At the end of the week we'll both go back to our separate lives. Like we always do."

Knowing what to expect should help keep her heart uninvolved. Sex. That's what this was. Nothing more.

"You're sure?" he asked, one last time. She probably should have taken the escape hatch, but she really didn't want it.

"Absolutely," she said, wrapping her arm around his neck and drawing him back down to her. "Love me. Now."

His eyes blazed. With a growl, he reached for her, rolling their bodies until she was draped across him, her soft curves sinking into his hard planes. She expected his hands to be rough, for him to tear at her clothes and skin and hair, to want to devour her as much as she wanted to be devoured.

Instead, he gently scraped the hair back from her face, staring up into her eyes for several moments. His eyes were sharp, missing nothing. With all of her clothes still on, somehow he managed to make her feel naked. Exposed. The intensity she could have handled, but this soul-deep exploration made her want to squirm.

Colt knew her better than anyone—including Wyn—and she realized she was about to share the only part of herself he hadn't already seen.

As if he'd read her mind Colt spoke, his gravel-roughened words brushing against her skin. "You're beautiful and he's an idiot."

She tried to capture his mouth, to cut off the words so that she wouldn't have to think about them, but he wouldn't let her.

"I don't want to talk about him while I'm having sex with you."

He rolled them, the unexpected motion leaving her breathless and slightly disoriented when the world stopped spinning around them.

"Who said anything about sex? *Sex* implies something raunchy and quick. Nothing about this is going to be quick. I'm going to touch every inch of you. Drive you mindless. Before I'm done you'll be begging me to let you come."

The secret muscles deep inside her body contracted at his words. She felt the slick proof that he could make good on his threat between her thighs. Lena squirmed, trying to relieve some of the pressure, but it didn't help. Nothing would.

"What if I make you beg first?" she asked, reaching between them. Her fingers had barely brushed against the tantalizing ridge of his erection before her hands were captured and stretched above her head.

"Maybe later."

She wanted to protest, but couldn't. Not with his mouth annihilating hers, stealing what coherent thought she had. The only thing left to do was feel.

He kept her locked there, at his mercy, as his mouth consumed everything it could touch. Pushing her thighs wide, he settled his own hips into the cradle there. The hard length of his erection pressed into the weeping center of her sex. Layers of clothing separated them, keeping what she really wanted so close but so far away.

As he worked slowly across her skin, stopping to suck and lick at pulse points she hadn't even known she had, he kept up a steady, torturous rocking motion. The hard heat of him rubbed against her, too light to bring her any sort of relief. It wasn't long before her head was thrashing between her upstretched arms, her eyes closed tight against the unforgiving edge of frustration.

Only when her body burned so hot she thought it might implode did he let go long enough to tug her clothes away. Any time she'd allowed herself to think about this moment, there had always been a tinge of anxiety. They'd been friends forever, but he'd never seen her naked. Would he be disappointed?

In reality, she was too consumed to worry about anything but the relief only he could give her.

Her eyes, gritty with need, watched as the sharp edge of his gaze scraped down the length of her body. Her back arched, begging him to put her out of her misery. Her breasts felt heavy and swollen. The tight nipples ached to feel the pebbled surface of his tongue caress them. The insides of her thighs were wet with desire, waiting, weeping, for him to finish this.

After all her blustering bravado, it didn't take long for her to beg. "Touch me. Please."

He did, this time leaving her hands free to return the favor. She reached for his clothes, tearing frantically until they finally fell away. Her hands shook as they skimmed down the warm expanse of his chest.

He was so solid beneath her touch, drawn tight with the same tension that whipped through her own body. The muscles beneath her fingers quivered. The further they dipped towards his sex the harder they leapt.

Her fingers feathered down the length of his erection and his entire body jerked. A low animal rumble ripped through his chest. She'd meant to play, to torture him the way he was making her mindless, but that intention disappeared the moment he sucked the tip of her aching breast deep into his mouth.

Her breath backed into her throat and the world around her blurred. Her fist closed tight around him, a reflexive reaction to find an anchor in the storm. He was hot and heavy in her hand.

Her palm slipped up and down his smooth weight. He felt wonderful and she could imagine the exquisite pleasure of him filling her deep inside. Her own hips pumped in unison with her motions, mimicking what she wanted.

Lifting her legs, she wrapped them around his waist. Her heels pressed into his flanks, her hand guiding him to the center of her need.

"Wait," he said, the single word garbled almost beyond recognition. She whimpered in protest as he fought against her hold on him. Until she realized he was reaching into the magic backpack, removing a shiny foil packet.

"Condom," he uttered, tearing into the packet and rolling the latex over his sex. She watched as the long, throbbing vein that ran the length of him disappeared beneath the opaque surface.

Grasping her hips, Colt pulled her back beneath him. The weight of his body pressed her into the blanket, grounding her in a way she'd never realized she wanted. Her body felt hot and light, ready to break apart into pieces and disappear. Colt was the only thing that gave her substance. Surrounded by wild jungle, he was the only thing that felt real.

Reaching down to spread her folds, his fingers slipped and slid, hitting her clit and making her arch against him. Cool air brushed across her exposed skin and her muscles contracted in anticipation.

Colt slid inside, slowly, deliberately, the heft of his sex stretching her. Filling her up. She gasped. Lifting her knees, she widened her thighs, taking all of him that she could.

Their eyes locked. Something deep in her chest tightened, something scary. But it was too late to go back now.

"Don't think we won't be talking about why you just happen to have condoms in that backpack," she whispered, trying to distract herself.

A broken chuckle erupted from his body. She could feel it everywhere, the vibrations echoing through where they joined. "Later." His mouth grabbed hers and he said again against her lips, "Much later."

The frenzy, held at bay for far too long, finally broke free. Their bodies slapped together, over and over, each trying to pull and push one last ounce of desire from their joining. Lena sunk her teeth into Colt's shoulder. The salty tang of his skin exploded across her tongue. His fingers dug into her hips, lifting her higher as he pounded in and out of her.

Lena's body bowed. Every muscle froze and then exploded into a quivering mass of delirium. Pleasure tore at her, breaking her into pieces and leaving behind a shell of what she'd been before.

Colt joined her, yelling so loudly that a bird in the branches above them startled. Flying away, it rained indignant squawks down on them. Lena barely heard them, focused as she was so totally on the rolling aftershocks that rocked through her body.

Deep inside, she could feel the speeding pulse where she and Colt joined. Collapsing beside her, Colt gathered her in his arms. She was coherent enough to realize they were shaking, his entire body quivering with long-denied release.

She had no idea how long they lay there. She should probably be feeling something. Panic maybe. Or remorse. Perhaps guilt. But she felt none of those things. She felt…right. As if there was nowhere else in the world she'd rather be than right here, tucked against Colt, satisfaction still rushing through her muscles.

Exhaustion stole across her. There would be plenty of time for regret. *Later,* she thought, and snuggled deeper.

COLT BOLTED AWAKE. Where was he? It took him a minute to remember. The jungle. With Lena. She stirred beside him, still asleep.

Sitting up, he looked around and cursed. Darkness had fallen, although a weak, watery light still managed to filter down through the canopy of leaves above them. It couldn't be all that late. Here, surrounded by dense trees, the light disappeared early. The jungle thinned closer to the resort. If they hurried, they might be able to make it out.

He didn't want to think about Lena's reaction if they couldn't. While sleeping out in the open didn't bother him, he was pretty sure it wouldn't be her first choice. Not when there was a soft, comfortable bed waiting for them.

If he hadn't been such a lust-fogged idiot.

"Lena, get up. We have to go," he whispered gently.

"Hmm," she mumbled and rolled onto her side. Thirty seconds later she sat straight up. Eyes wide, she looked around them. Her body sagged as she frowned. "Well, shit."

Colt chuckled. Her reaction could have been worse. Holding out her clothes he said, "As much as I hate to say this, you need to get dressed."

While he'd been gathering her clothes, he'd pulled his own on. Reaching down, he grabbed his pack. Zipping open a side pocket, he pulled out his cell phone. Illuminating the dark screen confirmed what he'd already feared, no signal. Who needed a cell tower in the middle of the jungle?

Apparently, they did.

At least the phone's display told him what time it was. Later than he'd hoped but earlier than he'd feared.

Scraping her hair away from her face, Lena said, "What now, Boy Scout?"

"We might be able to hike out of here. If we can get to the waterfall, the jungle won't be as dense. There's still enough light that if we find the path back to the resort we'll be fine."

"And if we don't?"

"Then I guess we sleep outside."

Lena's mouth twisted into a grimace but she didn't protest. Instead she gestured forward. "Lead the way, Lewis."

"Lewis?"

"If we're going to be forging our way through the jungle I get to be Clark."

Colt just shook his head. Most of the women he'd dated would be having hysterics by now. Not Lena. Nope, hysterics were a waste of time.

"I don't suppose you have a flashlight in there." She gestured to the pack he'd thrown across his shoulder. Lifting his hand, he showed her that he'd already pulled it out.

"What about a four-course meal?"

"Sorry, out of luck. But I promise to feed you the minute we get back to civilization."

"You'd better." She mock-glared.

Grasping her hand, he pulled her directly behind him. "Stay one step back. The darker it becomes the easier it'll be to get separated."

"Why do you get to go first? What if I want to lead?"

"Who's the Boy Scout?"

Her mouth crunched into a straight line. Her eyes blazed with indignation. Colt cut off the argument he could see coming. "Besides, this way you won't get hit with any stray branches."

And he'd be able to tackle any danger head-on, protecting her the best he could. If anyone was going to step off a cliff or startle a wild animal it was going to be him. He'd gotten them into this mess and if anything happened to her...

His chest constricted. His lungs fought to pull in enough air. Something seriously close to panic suffused his entire body. Clenching his hands into fists, Colt deliberately banned the thought from his mind.

They were fine.

8

THEY WERE LOST.

Darkness settled well and truly around them. The space that had seemed enchanting, lush and romantic just hours before quickly took on a sinister cast. Gone was the gentle sunlight filtering through the canopy of the trees. Instead, dim moonlight barely broke through, only to completely disappear before touching the ground.

Lena was cold, tired and hungry. The jungle was supposed to be hot, but apparently not at night. She fervently wished for the sun, not only for light but also for warmth. Wrapping her arms around her body, she really wished she'd worn longer shorts.

They walked silently, the only sound between them the rustling of the dry leaves and branches beneath their feet.

Something startled beside them. The bush to Lena's right erupted and a large bird, its multicolored feathers muted by the darkness, flew straight at her.

She screamed—it was a reflex she wasn't proud of,

but there it was—and ducked. The thing almost grazed the top of her head, her hair swirling in the wake of its passing. Angry sounds echoed back as it settled into the branches of another tree behind them.

Lena's hand covered her chest, hoping that the pressure would keep her heart from escaping along with the bird.

Colt was there beside her, his hands running over her body looking for any sign of damage.

"I'm fine," she croaked through a tight throat. Frowning, she tried again, "I'm fine, just startled," and was happy to hear no hesitation in the words this time.

Although her legs still felt a bit wobbly. Colt wrapped his arm around her waist and pulled her up. Lena was grateful for the support, but knew it couldn't last. Locking her knees, she said, "Look, admit it, we're stuck out here for the night. We need to find some shelter and stop wandering around aimlessly over unfamiliar terrain."

The flashlight Colt had trained towards the ground bounced up to hit his face at an eerie angle. It highlighted the sharp contours of his jaw and cheekbones, leaving large sections of his face in shadow. It made him look…austere, a word she never would have used to describe him before now.

"No, the path has to be close. If we can find it we can follow it out."

The flashlight between them flickered ominously.

Lena looked pointedly down. "We need to conserve battery power."

Colt's face tightened. "It isn't safe out here. I need

to get you back to the resort before something terrible happens."

Lena frowned. What the hell was wrong with him? Colt was usually the most levelheaded person in a crisis. Driving one-twenty down a country road might have been the stupidest thing the man had ever done, but getting himself out of the car, calling 911 and then applying his own tourniquet to his broken and bleeding leg before he passed out had taken nerves of steel.

Colt was a problem solver. A Boy Scout for heaven's sake.

Maybe she wasn't the only one who'd been scared out of her skull by that bird.

"Don't they teach you to stay put when you get lost? Besides, the only thing I'm in danger of is twisting my ankle because I can't see where I'm walking. It's late, Colt. I'm tired. We need to find someplace to sleep and then hike out in the morning."

She watched as his eyes roamed her face. No question, he wasn't happy, but even before he opened his mouth she knew she'd gotten through to him.

"All right. I remember seeing a cave behind the waterfall. I've been hearing the rumbling for the past few minutes. We'll find the cave, make camp and then leave at first light."

Lena's eyebrows beetled. She didn't hear anything. Taking a step sideways, she moved out of the shelter of Colt's body and finally heard it. His tall frame had apparently been blocking the sound.

"Great. Lead on."

Twenty minutes later they broke through the line

of trees surrounding the pool. Somewhere along the way they'd circled around, coming out about thirty feet closer to the falls than where they'd both left the clearing. No doubt they'd spent some of the past few hours walking parallel to the falls instead of directly toward them.

"Remind me to give you a compass for Christmas," she quipped. "You can keep it with your stash of condoms."

"Don't worry. I'll have one delivered from the mainland tomorrow."

"Why? We coming back out here?"

Colt spun suddenly on his heel. Lena collided with him. His arms steadied her even as they pulled her closer.

"Not on your life." His eyes blazed, not with passion but with determination and fire. His fingers gripped her upper arms, digging almost painfully into her skin. She tried to move, but realized she couldn't even wiggle. "Promise me you'll never do something like this again."

"Like what? Go hiking? Have a picnic? Get lost? I can promise you I'll try."

Colt's jaw worked back and forth, his molars grinding tightly against each other.

Lena took a slow step closer and said quietly, "Colt, let go. You're hurting me."

His hands burst away from her body. She rocked slightly, surprised by the sudden loss of his support.

Spinning away, he raked his hands through his hair, leaving it disheveled and standing on end. "I'm sorry," he said, still facing away. "I'm just…worried. I can't believe I let this happen!" he roared.

She was finally beginning to understand.

"You let this happen?" she asked slowly. "I don't remember you being the only adult in this situation. Why are you to blame for us getting lost?"

Spinning back to her, he barked, "Because you're my responsibility."

That had her back up within seconds. "No, I'm not. I'm responsible for myself and have been for years, you idiot." Lena stalked closer, jabbing a finger into his chest. With each step she took forward, he took one back. "I don't remember blaming you for this predicament. Or wailing like some helpless female."

"I didn't mean…" he sputtered, backtracking nice and fast…straight into the water. One second he was standing in front of her, the next he was sprawled in knee-deep water, his eyes round and bright with surprise.

Lena's first reaction was to jump in after him. Uncaring that her shoes were now soaking wet, she splashed into the water and crouched down beside him. "Are you okay?"

She reached for him, tugging uselessly at the weight of his body. Instead of answering, he reached beneath her arms and toppled her into the water beside him. The water was shockingly warm, the pool shallow enough to have heated through from the sun.

They grappled in the water, each trying to get the upper hand. She knew it was useless, but refused to give up without a fight. After several minutes, Colt ended up above her, her legs pinned down by the weight of his hips and her arms held loosely in his hands.

He grinned down at her, wicked and mischievous.

"Great, now my clothes are soaked. I don't suppose you have a spare set in the pack?"

"Sure," he said. "For me."

"You're going to have to share. I'm already cold, and wet clothes won't help."

He ground his hips slowly against her, making a warm ribbon of need wind slowly through her body.

"I'm sure we can come up with a better way to keep you warm."

"Oh, yeah," she countered, arching her back and pressing the wet globes of her breasts against the warm expanse of his chest.

Desire, strong and hard, zinged between them. She wanted him again. She wanted to feel him moving inside her, stretching her body and filling her up. She wanted to touch him, taste him and learn what she could do to make those little growling noises erupt from his throat again.

And here was as good a place as any. Reaching between them, she wiggled her hand closer to the burgeoning ridge of his cock. But she didn't get there in time.

Instead, Colt pushed away from her. Drops of water rained down around her as he stood, reaching to help her up after him.

"I was talking about building a fire," he said, a teasing grin playing at the corners of his mouth.

"Bastard," she grumbled, suppressing her own smile.

She took a step away, but Colt pulled her back, jerking her into his arms and stealing her breath with a kiss. She went under, happily, letting him take whatever he wanted. Opening herself, body, mind, soul to him.

The clearing around them was quiet. And while the jungle they'd hiked through had seemed dark and dangerous, the waterfall and pool somehow held a tinge of magic. Even the massive roar of the water as it crashed over the edge only reminded her what the power of letting go could provide—deep, reverberating pleasure.

Maybe being lost wasn't so bad after all. Not if she was lost with Colt.

Lena was all ready for round two. Who needed an emergency blanket when the sandy shore beneath their feet was available? She tried to wiggle away from Colt, to work her hands between them enough so that she could fill her palms with the rolling waves of muscle that crossed his tight abs.

But instead of reacting to her touch, Colt stilled. It was unnatural, his sudden and complete lack of motion. Even his lungs stopped sucking in air.

Lena looked up into his face. "Colt?" His arms tightened, but his gaze was no longer focused on her.

Turning her head slowly, Lena followed his line of sight and nearly screamed.

"Don't move," he whispered.

A large cat, black as the center of the jungle, crouched across from them.

"What is that?" she whispered.

"Jaguar. I think."

It was lapping up water from the pool, somehow

managing to never take its stalking, steady gaze off them. It paused, the whites of its eyes flashing as if realizing it was no longer the only one watching.

Even from this distance, Lena could see the powerful muscles of its flanks. They quivered, as if gathered in readiness to spring at any moment.

"I wonder if it's hungry," she whispered wryly.

It stared at them. Lena could count the seconds by the racing thud of Colt's heartbeat next to her own. The cat's dark pink tongue licked, lightning-fast, over its maw.

"I don't think that's a good sign," Colt rumbled.

Lena felt the tight coil of Colt's muscles as he braced for fight or flight. A bolt of awareness—ill-timed and seriously unhelpful—blasted through her body. She jerked against him, unable to stop herself from the bone-deep reaction. Colt felt it, his body stirring against hers.

As if sensing their distraction, the cat took that moment to disappear. They caught the flash of tail as it slipped into the jungle. If they hadn't known it was there, the twitch could have been just a shadow.

Galvanized into motion, Colt set her away, pulling her out of the water behind him. Her body protested the loss of his heat, but she understood. He was in a flurry, gathering sticks, leaves and moss. Pushing the mess into her arms, he went back for more, this time searching for larger chunks of wood.

She assumed the paraphernalia was for a fire. He proved her right when he directed her across the pool toward the waterfall and said, "We'll build a fire at the entrance. It'll keep us warm and keep that guy away."

A shiver of a different sort raced up her spine.

Her waterlogged shoes sunk into the sand at the bottom of the pool. The closer they got to the falls the harder it became to lift each foot.

Colt stopped in front of her. With a curt "Wait here," he disappeared through the wall of water protecting the entrance to the cave.

A protest sputtered on Lena's lips even as she realized it was pointless. Stupid man. If he encountered something dangerous in there he'd be fighting alone.

Wrapping her body around the fire-starting materials to keep them as dry as possible, she followed behind him.

She let out a gasp as the water washed down over her back. She might already be wet, but the water cascading down was much cooler than that of the collecting pool.

The place was dark. Lena looked around, frantically searching for the telltale shine of Colt's flashlight.

"Colt," she yelled.

There was no answer.

She tried again, lifting her voice and spinning around in the dark cavern. "Colt!" The only thing that came back was an empty echo.

"DAMMIT, I TOLD YOU to stay put."

Colt tried to ignore Lena's jump of surprise as he walked up behind her. After sweeping the cave to make sure it wasn't already occupied, he'd switched off the flashlight and let his eyes become adjusted.

His heart had pounded every second they'd been separated, but leaving her alone outside had been the lesser of two evils. Without knowing what was inside the cave, bringing her with him had been too much of a risk. The confined space wouldn't have provided many options for escape or fight.

As it turned out, the cave was empty. The ceiling at the front opened high above their heads, but it sloped downward to connect with the floor about twenty yards back.

For the first time since he'd awoken to find the jungle darkening around them, Colt let out a sigh of relief. At least here they'd be safe until morning.

Lena's eyes shimmered through darkness, twin beacons of light that pulled him closer. The smell of her, wild and wet, slammed through him. The primitive urge to have her, to prove to himself that she was unharmed and safe, overwhelmed him. He jerked her forward, crushing her against his body. The heat of her singed his skin. He swore he could hear the sizzle as the water on his skin turned to steam.

Her breath whooshed out to tickle across the damp cotton of his shirt. His arms wrapped around her, plastering her to him as tightly as their wet clothes clung to them.

His heart pounded against his rib cage like an angry bird fighting to get out. He was certain she must be able to feel it, too. His teeth ground together in the back of his mouth, a last-ditch attempt to find some shred of control.

Somewhere in the back of his mind, Colt realized he was heading for disaster. Out here, something dark inside him had been released—the urge to protect and dominate, to claim what was his and to never let it go.

It was a side of himself he wasn't completely enamored with but couldn't seem to fight. Not with Lena standing in front of him, the dark centers of her eyes watching, waiting, the low guttural words of her taunt egging him on. "Take me."

With a growl of surrender—to her, to himself, to whatever this was—Colt erupted around her. He claimed her lips in a frenzy of passion. His tongue plundered her mouth, but she met him thrust for thrust, scraping and jabbing and asking for more.

She sucked him deeper inside, so far that he could feel the vibration of her mewl of approval.

His hands scraped against her scalp, burrowing in her hair and angling her mouth so he could get more of her. His arm wrapped around her back, lifting her up off the floor so she had nowhere else to go but to him.

She didn't fight against the tempest blowing between them. Instead, she opened to him, giving everything and taking even more in return. What they'd shared before had been slow and tender, the final capitulation of two people who'd cared about each other for a long time. This was a scrabbling fight for the ecstasy only they could give each other.

Her legs, left with nothing else to do but dangle, found purchase around his waist. She arched into his hold, rubbing the heat of her sex against his throbbing erection.

Colt fought the sensation that he was drowning, swamped not only by his emotions for Lena, but by her unquestioning surrender and trust in him. Trust that he would keep her safe.

A cloud of passion wrapped them together, blocking out everything else. All he wanted to do was feel her, taste her, absorb her into his body so he'd never forget this moment of possessing her. In the days and weeks to come, when the inevitable happened and they returned to their real lives, he'd still have this memory to take with him into dark, lonely nights.

And he was bound and determined to make the most of it.

Oblivious to everything except his need for her, Colt stumbled backwards until Lena's back connected with the rough stone wall. She arched against him, letting out a tiny sound. He tried to pull away, but her fingers scrabbled against his shoulders and a low growl of protest vibrated between their lips.

Her legs gripped him tighter, her ankles digging mercilessly into his back to bring him closer.

He pulled back long enough to look into her eyes, deep, dark and smoldering. Her thigh muscles squeezed around him, raising and lowering her body in a caress that nearly drove him to his knees.

The feel of her, wild and restless in his arms, was something he'd never allowed himself to want. And now, he was sorely afraid he'd never get enough.

Ripping at the hem of her shirt, Colt tore it up over

her head and threw it into the yawning mouth of the
cave behind them. She took the opportunity to do the
same with his. The wet plop of his shirt against stone
was somehow satisfying.

Her soft lips settled against his skin. He felt as if
he were on fire, but the heat of her tongue as it licked
across his throat was still hard to miss. She pulled at
him, sucking him inside and sending sheets of light-
ning dancing across his skin.

His own mouth clamped hard and fast around the
begging center of her breast. She tasted sweet—like
tropical fruit after a cool rain—as he rolled the tight
nipple beneath the swell of his tongue. Intoxicating,
that's what she was.

Colt ran his hands up the length of her thighs, trying
to find a way in beneath the taut cloth of her shorts. He
could feel her damp center pressed against him, taunting him with the promise of wet heat. He wanted it, but
he didn't want to let her go.

Finally, with a growl of frustration answered by a
peal of feminine laughter, Colt tumbled them both to
the hard stone floor.

She arched into his waiting body, and he relished the
heat as they collided. Skin on skin, their damp bodies
clung. She reached between them, opening the catch on
her shorts. He hissed as the back of her hand caressed
the bulge of his erection, a torturous caress that was
hardly enough.

Her lips curved into a smile she failed to suppress.
"Witch," he breathed against those lips before he nipped
gently at the corners, punishing them for their taunt.

Together, they rolled across the floor, an undulating mass of legs, arms and heated bodies. Somewhere in the middle of the melee they managed to push their remaining clothes out of the way. Colt's legs were hobbled, tied together by the material neither of them could be bothered to deal with. Lena's shorts dangled from one ankle, the one she managed to wedge high up his hip.

They came to rest, Colt's back propped against the wall, Lena straddling his lap. Her thighs were spread wide, feet propped behind him, the swollen flesh of her sex open and waiting. He wanted to taste and touch, to explore every inch.

Colt reached between them, slipping his fingers deep into the heat of Lena's body. She gasped, contracting around the invasion. Her hips surged forward, pulling him deeper.

Her head fell back in abandon. His fingers flexed, widening her channel and pushing against the force of the tension building inside her. Slowly, he dragged them back out again to the very edge. Her whimper of protest quickly morphed into a moan of pleasure when he slammed in again.

He tortured them both, watching as her body took him over and over again. The slippery evidence of her desire coated his hand. She quivered around him. He could practically feel the crank of tension as it twisted inside her. She was so close.

His cock throbbed with an insistent demand that he was powerless to ignore. Pulling his hand from her body, he swallowed her protest with his mouth. Grasping her hips, he pulled her up and brought her down onto his hard length.

She screamed with pleasure, the echo reverberating around them tenfold. He surged beneath her, driving every last inch into her welcoming depths. The feel of her muscles contracting, trying to hold him in place even as he pulled out for another thrust was exquisite.

Skin on skin, they crashed together over and over again. Rough rock bit into Colt's back. Lena's fingers bored into his shoulders, trying to find a purchase. Her face pressed into the crook of his neck, each panting wail of her pleasure bursting deep inside his chest.

He felt her fall, knew the moment her body let go. The rolling waves of her release started deep inside, ripping up his shaft and quaking through her entire body. Colt felt the answering surge start at the base of his spine, an explosion of ectasy that had the world around them going even blacker.

The increasingly powerful swells of bliss left him breathless, floundering, as they washed repeatedly across him. His arms tightened around Lena, holding her to him. She was the only solid thing in the universe.

She collapsed onto his chest, her body limp and spent. Part of him relished knowing he'd done that to her, brought her that kind of devastating pleasure.

Above him, her chest continued to heave, fighting to catch her breath. Aftershocks burst through her body, making her quiver and contracting her walls around his spent sex. It felt right, this connection they'd found deep in the heart of the jungle.

And then he realized what they'd done.

"We didn't use anything," he said through a dry throat.

"What?" she mumbled sleepily against his chest.

Panic shot through him. "We didn't use a condom."

9

LENA TRIED TO SIT UP, to move away from Colt and what they'd just done, but the steel bands of his arms kept her tight against him. She could still feel the pulse of him buried deep inside her. She wanted to be upset—with herself and with him—but she couldn't be.

They'd both gotten carried away, neither of them taking time to think rationally.

Panic rushed through her blistering and hard. *She* hadn't thought rationally. She knew better than to let hormones and emotions overwhelm her that way.

But, apparently, that was difficult for her to do with Colt around. He broke through all of her barriers, pulling at pieces of her she'd never wanted to admit existed. No one, no man, had ever made her feel so deliriously out of control.

And the fact that she'd liked it just made it that much worse.

Colt stirred beneath her, picking her up and gently placing her onto the cool floor. He towered above her, staring down with shuttered eyes. She really wished she knew what he was thinking, but she couldn't read him. Not now.

Pushing up to her own feet, Lena crossed her arms over her breasts. She realized it was a pointless gesture, but she did it anyway.

"I'm on the pill."

"Oh," he said, his voice flat. "That's good."

Turning on his heel, Colt silently gathered the branches they'd brought in with them. Reaching into his pack, he pulled out a box of matches. The tiny flare of light hissed through the quiet cave.

Lena shivered. Gathering her clothes, she was about to pull the damp material over her head when Colt stopped her.

"Spread them out over here to dry." Reaching back into the pack again, he pulled out a T-shirt and handed it to her. Their fingers brushed, and the now-familiar sizzle of need flashed up her arm. Colt jerked his hand away.

And she mourned for the sense of closeness they'd shared a few minutes before.

"We also had blood tests for the marriage license, if that's what you're worried about."

Fire caught, stuttered and then flared between them. Colt pulled on a pair of nylon gym shorts that must have also come from the pack. Across the flames, his eyes flashed. Something quick, hard and bright, but before Lena could figure out what it was it was gone.

"It never crossed my mind, Lena. I know you better than that."

"Maybe, but Wyn was certainly promiscuous enough for all of us."

"Something tells me that sex wasn't on your agenda for the past few months."

What the heck was that supposed to mean? "How the hell do you know that?"

He stepped closer, the red-orange glow of flames washing across his bare chest. His voice took on an intimate timbre. "Let's just say, you don't respond like a woman who's been well-satisfied."

For perverse reasons she didn't understand even as she said it, she countered, "Wyn is a great lover, thank you very much."

Colt's lips twitched, not with humor but something far darker. "I'm sure your cousin would agree."

She drew in a breath, as if the barb had actually connected with her chest.

"What about you? How many lovers have you had in the last year? Ten? Twenty?"

"I like sex."

"You may like it—and I'll be the first to admit you're pretty damn good at it—but that doesn't make you a god among men. What it makes you is pathetic and lonely. When's the last time you had a real relationship, Colt? Not some one-night stand but something meaningful? Something built on a level beyond the physical?"

Colt's mouth thinned and he took another menacing step toward her. Instead of taking the hint and backing away, she moved closer, going toe-to-toe.

"You don't know what you're talking about."

"The hell I don't. I watched you self-destruct after you lost your parents. And when that didn't cure the pain, you shut everyone out of your life."

"You're still here."

She scoffed. "Please. I get random phone calls. A long weekend here and there. That's not a relationship, that's convenience."

"That's my job!" he hollered, his voice rising with frustration that matched her own.

How had they gone so quickly from total bliss to this?

"A convenient excuse, Colt. You immersed yourself in your work, using it as a barrier to distance you from everyone and everything that matters. You insulated yourself in the hopes that it would keep you from being hurt."

She saw pain flash across Colt's face and immediately regretted her words. They were true, but that didn't give her the right to throw them at him like expletives.

Reaching for him, she tried to apologize. "Colt, I'm sorry." He shook her off.

Closing the conversation completely, Colt said, "We'd better get some sleep while we can."

Spreading the emergency blanket out on the cave floor, he lay down, gesturing for her to join him. She was surprised when he wrapped his arm around her waist and pulled her tight against his chest.

Tension still clung to his muscles; she could feel the hard coil of them pressing into her back. But he was touching her. At the moment she'd take what she could get.

Squeezing her eyes shut, Lena tried to will her body and mind to sleep, but it didn't help. After a while, she thought he must have dozed off. Until he whispered, "I was…"

"Worried."

"Scared."

Lena realized that sometime while they'd lain there, wrapped together, the tension had left his body. He'd relaxed behind her, his voice sounding drowsy and thick.

"Not sure I'm ready for that responsibility. Tiny little thing dependent on you for everything. Too fragile." The steel band of his arms pressed against her lungs. She didn't think he knew what he was doing. "Bad enough you almost got hurt."

She wanted to argue with him, to protest that she'd come nowhere close to getting hurt. But she realized it wouldn't do any good. Not just because he wouldn't have listened, but also because he was already asleep.

"OH, THANK GAWD," greeted them when they exited the jungle the next morning. Waking at dawn hadn't been difficult since the hard stone floor hadn't made a very comfortable bed.

Georgie, tears glistening in her eyes, broke through a group of people who'd gathered at the head of the path. Throwing her arms around Lena's shoulders, the petite blonde squeezed her hard before pushing her away. "You scared us half to death."

Wesley appeared behind her, gently pulling her away.

Marcy came next, two tall men Lena had never seen before quick on her heels. She wore an expression that was probably meant to intimidate, but Lena was too happy to see Marcy's efficient face to pay attention.

"What happened?" she asked, her stern tone ruined by the tremor of relief she couldn't hide.

The men, one with hair as dark as the jungle had been, the other bright and blond, followed her. The dark-haired one studied them both, his sharp gaze missing nothing. He didn't speak, but there was no missing the air of authority that clung to him.

The blond, who looked as if he should have a surfboard tucked beneath his arm, put his hand on Marcy's shoulder. Lena wasn't sure if it was in warning or support, but either way she didn't let it sit there long. Shaking him off, she asked, "Are you both all right?"

"We're fine," Colt answered.

"Tired and hungry, but no worse for wear. We… um…got distracted."

A titter went up from the crowd that had gathered behind Marcy and her mystery men.

Colt spoke up when embarrassment made Lena's words falter. "Before we knew it, dark was falling. We couldn't get out so we camped in the cave behind the waterfall."

"You two are damn lucky," the tall blond interjected.

Colt just nodded his head.

"Well." Turning on her heel towards the gathered group, Marcy clapped her hands and said, "It looks like we won't be needing your help after all. Everyone can return to his or her previous schedule."

There were several shouts of "Glad you're back" and "Happy you're safe" as the group broke apart and melted away.

Wesley pulled gently at Georgie's elbow, trying to get her to follow him down the path. She reluctantly did, yelling over her shoulder, "You have to tell me everything when you're feeling better. I was so worried."

Left with Marcy and the men, Lena felt exhaustion envelop her. It had been a long, emotion-filled night.

The blond man stepped forward, finally introducing himself. "I'm Simon, the owner. This is Zane, our head of security." The other man jerked his head up in silent acknowledgment of the introduction, but didn't bother to speak.

"If you need anything, let Marcy know. If you'll excuse me, I need to get back to my office. I'm glad to know you're safe."

Without waiting for their response, the men spun on their heels and disappeared. Marcy stared after them, a frown tugging at her mouth. Looking back at them she said, "I'm sorry for Simon's abrupt departure."

"No, really, it's fine," Colt said. "We're actually very tired. We could probably sleep for the rest of the day."

Marcy's frown deepened, digging grooves between her eyebrows. "Well, we already lost all of yesterday. When I realized you'd slipped away I rescheduled several things for today. I suppose we could push most of them to tomorrow." She studied them for several seconds. "Would you feel up to something tonight?"

Lena looked across at Colt. He shrugged.

"All right. We'll be ready tonight," she offered. After all, it was their fault the photo shoot was so far behind.

"Excellent. I'll send Mikhail to get you around seven. Come hungry," Marcy said, her eyes sparkling.

Together, Lena and Colt stumbled across the resort, pausing long enough to change out of their rumpled clothes before falling into bed. She couldn't speak for Colt, but she was asleep almost instantly.

SEVERAL HOURS LATER, Lena stirred awake, arching her body in a stretch before she even opened her eyes. Colt watched her, as he'd been doing for the past several minutes.

Sometime yesterday Marcy had returned their bungalow to its former state, including putting the standard-issue cotton sheets back on the bed. The crisscross pattern had imprinted into Lena's skin, marring her cheek in an endearing way that made him want to kiss her, slowly and deliberately.

Had it only been yesterday that he'd first claimed her? It seemed like days, years ago, instead of less than twenty-four hours. But thinking about their brief history made him realize they hadn't made love in a bed. Nice, comfortable mattress, soft sheets, no bugs or birds or leaves or rocks.

The insatiable exhaustion was gone, replaced with a languid awareness. And suddenly he wanted to push her deep into that plush mattress and leave the imprint of their joined bodies there. Reaching toward her, Colt brushed his fingers gently down her spine. A smile curved her mouth, but her eyes stayed shut.

His lips feathered against her bare shoulder, the tiny strap of the gown she'd thrown on slipping down her arm. She rolled over into his arms, her bleary eyes opening to reveal the unhurried heat that smoldered there.

She hummed deep in her throat as his fingers trailed lightly over her chest. The soft material of her gown slipped across her skin beneath his touch, arousing them both. A single fingernail snagged on the telltale tent of her peaked nipple.

She pushed into him, silently asking for more.

But before he could give it to her, a loud knock sounded on the door. With a curse, Colt looked at the clock and realized it was already six. How could they have slept the entire day away?

Another knock sounded at the door. Colt yelled, "We have an hour." A chuckle was the only response.

While he wasn't looking, Lena had scooted off the other side of the bed. He tried to reach for her, but she twisted away. "No way, buddy. You might not care what I look like in these photographs, but I do. I haven't showered since yesterday. I fell in a pond, slept on the ground and desperately need to condition my hair."

"You look beautiful," he countered.

"Said the man sporting the rather impressive erection."

Lena's lips twitched. Colt looked down, although it wasn't as if he needed proof. He could feel the pulsing ache all the way to his toes. In that split second, she slipped into the bathroom, cutting off any thought of him following inside when the lock clicked loudly behind her.

Colt wanted to be upset, but couldn't muster up the energy. The wait was worth it when she emerged a half hour later, her skin glowing beneath the warm earth tones of the dress she'd put on.

Colt would have reached for her then, but the shake of her head stopped him. Not to mention the pointed finger she leveled at the still steamy bathroom. Being surrounded by the scent of her shampoo while he showered was torture of the highest degree.

A low, steady strum took up residence deep in his blood. It was relentless, this need for her that had settled into his bones. No matter how many times he had her, he wanted her again. Immediately, as often as possible. He was beginning to fear that need could never be met.

For the first time since he'd convinced himself he could have her, he wondered what would happen when they left. He'd promised himself they'd go their separate ways, but what if he couldn't do it? What if one week with her wasn't enough?

"You almost ready?" she called, cutting off his line of thought before it took him someplace he didn't want to go.

Walking outside together, they were greeted by Mikhail, who grinned knowingly. Colt felt the urge to knock the expression right off his face, but fought against it. Instead, they followed him down a path and out onto the beach.

A white canvas tent had been set up along the deserted stretch. Colt could hear the laughter of other guests farther back toward the resort, but here the place had an untouched, primitive quality that appealed to him.

Beside him, Lena twined her arm through his. He could feel the way her whole body quivered. He wondered if she was nervous and then realized nerves had nothing to do with it when she looked up at him. Her eyes glowed with anticipation, excitement and a knowing expectation that he had every intention of fulfilling at the first opportunity.

Mikhail slipped ahead of them. Colt held the flap open so Lena could enter. Marcy, Mikhail and his crew waited.

He had to admit that Marcy had gone above and beyond the call of duty. The tent was made of lightweight canvas. Even if she'd had it up all day, it wouldn't have absorbed as much of the sun as some other fabrics might have. Piles of pillows were thrown around the intimate space that centered around a low table barely a foot or two off the ground.

A sea of silver-covered dishes sat on the table, waiting to be revealed. He wondered what was inside and figured he'd find out soon enough. He expected stuffed grape leaves and dripping baklava. Instead, when someone from the crew stepped forward, she exposed trays of tropical fruit, shrimp, oysters, skewers of chicken and beef with sweet-smelling chili sauce and an assortment of finger-size desserts that made his mouth water.

Lena dropped to her knees in front of the table, staring in wonder at the spread before her. Looking over her shoulder at the woman standing at the entrance to the tent, she said, "Marcy, you didn't have to go to all this trouble."

"Yes, I did. The shot has to be perfect. I want to feature it in a two-page spread."

Some of the wonder disappeared from Lena's eyes and Colt wanted to admonish Marcy for ruining the moment for her.

Apparently realizing what she'd just done, Marcy took a step forward, reaching out to Lena. "I'm sorry, that didn't come out the way I meant it to. I didn't do this just for you, but I do want you to enjoy it. I've seen some of the preliminary pictures. Trust me, you've earned it. They're amazing and people will be flocking to Escape in no time because of them. I owe you."

Lena smiled up at the other woman. "Well, this is certainly a great way to start. This is wonderful, Marcy. You've thought of everything."

Even double-layering a soft rug across the bottom of the tent so that neither of them would end the night rolling around in the sand. For that, Colt was eternally grateful.

"I try." Marcy's cheeks flushed with satisfaction. "I'm going to let Mikhail get to work. He has instructions to leave you alone once he's got what he needs."

Colt dropped to the pillows on the opposite side of the table thinking about how perfect this was and hoping Mikhail would finish quickly.

Mikhail entered as Marcy left. He surveyed them both, asked Lena to angle her legs differently and positioned Colt's shoulders more squarely toward the camera. But on the whole, he seemed satisfied with the scene.

Colt looked down at the food and realized for the first time that there weren't any utensils. Everything on the table was designed to be eaten with their hands. Marcy really had thought of everything.

Shaking his head in awe, Colt reached for a morsel of something and held it out toward Lena. She paused for a second, reaching for her own bite, but instead leaned against the table and opened her mouth. She sucked the food from his hand, her pink tongue licking across the underside of his fingers. His eyes narrowed as a spike of need stabbed straight through him.

Picking up a shrimp, he reached for her hand, closed her fingers around it and brought it up to his own lips. Two could play that game. He relished the way her eyes flashed as his tongue lapped the sauce from her fingers. He practically swallowed the thing whole, grateful it was small, so that he could chase a drop as it slipped down her wrist.

"So good," he breathed against her skin. He licked across the sensitive veins there, enjoying the way her fingers curled and her pulse jumped.

In the background, Colt could hear the whir of the shutter and the click of the button as Mikhail caught shot after shot. He ignored the other man, instead focusing solely on Lena and building the tension and desire between them.

He slipped around the corner of the table, moving closer to her. She was up on her knees, leaning toward him, waiting for him to feed her something else.

He picked up a pastry shell filled with a spiced rice mixture. Tipping it to her mouth, he waited for her to take a bite. The crunch of the broken shell echoed through the space, but his eyes were drawn to the curve of her neckline and the dark hollow between her breasts. A few grains of rice had slipped free, rolling down her skin to disappear.

Colt leaned forward, ready to dive in after them but Mikhail's loud throat-clearing stopped him. Instead, Lena wiggled her body and dress till the stray grains fell free. He had to admit watching her gyration was almost as good as retrieving them himself.

They fed each other, drank sweet wine from crystal flutes and laughed at the mess they both made of the beautiful meal. Their fingers grazed, their bodies touched and while they started out on opposite sides of the table Lena was soon practically sitting in Colt's lap.

Colt wasn't sure when Mikhail left. He was aware of the man's departure in some foggy corner of his mind because at that moment he'd been freed to do everything that he wanted, no longer obligated to hold back in deference to the audience or the lens. When he'd left, Mikhail had had the foresight to close the single flap to give them some privacy. Colt was glad the other man had thought of it, because he was too far gone.

One hunger slaked and another stoked so high that both of them feared being consumed by the flames. They pushed back from the table and rolled together onto the pile of soft pillows.

Lena's dress twisted around her thighs. He wanted

to see her, all of her, spread out before him. Lifting her up into his arms, he peeled the garment from her body.

His breath backed into his throat when he realized she wasn't wearing anything beneath. All night, she'd been naked under the thin layer of fabric and he hadn't known it. He was still sane enough to realize perhaps that was a good thing. If he had known, he might not have been able to control himself long enough to let Mikhail get what he needed.

"What have you done with my practical Lena?" he asked as his fingers glided down the smooth expanse of her inner thigh.

Her eyes smoldered, an intensity that drove deep down into his soul and twisted. "I didn't put on any panties, Colt. It's not like I organized a bra-burning or chained myself to the door of some industrial giant. I figured why bother if they were just coming off."

His lips trailed across the dip of her stomach, his tongue swirling into her navel. "There she is."

"What's wrong with practical?" she stuttered as his knee nudged against her own. He relished the view of her swollen flesh as she opened for him.

"Nothing," he growled. "Practical is good, especially if it makes touching you easier."

The heady scent of her arousal swirled around them. He took a deep breath, holding it inside so he could re-member this moment forever.

With one hand he parted her folds, sinking in and swiping his tongue across the warm surface of her sex. She tasted like heaven, and he wanted more.

She bucked beneath him, pressing against his mouth.

She was so hot and wet. Her sex burned around the invasion of his tongue as he drove relentlessly in and out. His lips clamped tightly over the jutting nub of her clit, sucking hard in a way that had breath bursting from her body in frantic pants.

Before he could spear a finger inside and suck her to orgasm, she reared up beneath him, bucking him off. Colt sprawled backward into the pillows. Lena rose above him, the tangled mass of her dark mahogany hair running riotously down her back.

Her eyes smoldered. A tempting smile teased across her lips. Colt tried to sit up, but a single hand on his shoulder pressed him back down.

"My turn," she said, pressing her mouth to the flat plane of his stomach. Colt enjoyed the happy leap of the muscles where she touched. Her mouth slid close and his cock jumped.

She laughed, a low-throated sound that had air brushing torturously across him. She didn't keep him suspended in misery long. Her tongue quickly followed, licking slowly from tip to base. Her hand teased across the swollen orbs below as she sucked him deep into her throat. The moist heat was maddening, but not nearly as perfect as being buried deep inside her body.

She slid back and forth and he let her play, until he couldn't take anymore. Pulling her away, he spun them both, pressing her hard into the soft floor.

"Please tell me you were practical and brought condoms," she panted.

Her nails scraped down his chest, leaving red welts as he reached behind her to grab the condom he'd stuffed into the pocket of his pants. She flicked one of his erect nipples, making his stomach contract with pleasure.

Snatching the packet from his fingers, she tore through the foil. The combination of her warmth and the tight latex as she rolled it down over his aching cock had him hissing through his teeth.

He pulled from her grasp. Spreading her thighs wide, he plunged deep inside. She was so hot and ready, welcoming. Her gasp of pleasure blasted through him even as her sex wrapped so tightly around him that he could barely breathe.

"Oh g-god…" she stuttered as he moved inside her.

He pulsed in and out—quick, shallow, deep. Lena's head thrashed against the pillows. Incoherent whimpers fell from her parted lips. Her hips pumped, grinding against his.

One second she was straining, reaching for the same exquisite moment as he was. The next she was wild beneath him. Her body, poised on the edge, flew apart. Bucking, quaking, sobbing, her orgasm was more than he could take. Her milking muscles gripped him in a hard fist, refusing to let him go.

The power of his own release crashed over him in warm waves, blocking everything but the feel of her from his brain. Each time was stronger, better, more powerful than the last, than anything he'd experienced before.

How was he ever going to live without this? Without her?

Lena collapsed beneath him. Her legs and arms

sprawled uselessly. He had just enough brainpower left to realize he was going to crush her. Rolling them both one last time, he draped her spent body across his.

Her hair spilled over his chest and her nose buried deep into the crook of his neck. She burrowed against him, as if she were trying to get inside his skin as the last and only joining they hadn't actually been able to accomplish.

And he was happy to have her there. As close as they could possibly get.

Colt wrapped his arms around her and held on. He didn't want to let her go.

But he would have to. Because everything ended, even this.

10

A BRIGHT BEAM OF SUNLIGHT sliced across Lena's face, pulling her from the most delicious dream. Sometime during the night they'd stumbled back to their bungalow. Grumbling, she cursed their preoccupation and lack of foresight—neither she nor Colt had thought to draw the curtains.

"What time is it?" Colt croaked out, his head buried beneath a pillow.

Squinting against the glare, Lena rummaged on the bedside table until the bright red numbers on the clock came into view.

"Nine."

Colt sat bolt upright in bed. "Crap! We have to get ready."

Lena frowned at him. "Ready for what?" If her memory served, they didn't have anything planned until later in the day. She had to admit that while she'd been a little trepidatious about the whole photo-session thing, it actually hadn't been that bad.

A smile Lena couldn't hold in stretched across her lips. Especially last night...

"I have a surprise," Colt said, his lips and words brushing across her naked shoulder.

She narrowed her eyes. "You know I don't like surprises." Her whole life, *Surprise!* was usually followed by *We're moving to*...fill in the blank. L.A., Chicago, London, Geneva, Bangkok, whatever. No, she didn't appreciate surprises. The word alone had the ability to send dread and panic through her body.

"You like *my* surprises."

"When have you ever surprised me?"

"That time I showed up on your doorstep when I was supposed to be in Kenya."

Oh, yeah. She did remember that. The first year out of college had been difficult for her. She'd hated her job writing bad copy for a third-rate marketing firm. Her apartment had sucked and no one in the building seemed interested in making new friends. She'd been lonely, but had tried to hide it from Colt whenever he managed to call. He'd been so excited about the project he was working on.

That conversation, she must have failed miserably because two days later he was on her doorstep, a bottle of wine in one hand and a fistful of movies in the other. Granted, he'd brought shoot-'em-up, world-destruction, epic adventures instead of chick flicks. But spending those two days together had made a huge difference in her disposition.

A few months later she'd gone to work at Rand doing

graphic design—what she'd wanted to be doing in the first place—met Wyn and everything had changed.

For the first time, Lena wondered what would have happened the next time Colt came home if she hadn't been dating someone. That weekend, something had felt different, but she'd convinced herself it was all the changes in her life, not how she felt about Colt. Would all the sparks flying now have erupted then?

"Okay, so I reluctantly give you the opportunity to surprise me. But I retain my right to balk at any time."

"Trust me, you won't." With a mischievous glint running through his bright green eyes, Colt scooted off the bed, grasping the covers and dragging them with him.

The entire knot—comforter, sheets, pillows—fell with a plop to the floor leaving her totally naked. Two days ago she probably would have squealed, made some ineffectual attempt to cover up and then quickly disappeared. Today, she simply stretched, arching her body toward him.

"No fair," he growled, his eyes going dark and dangerous as they traveled up the length of her body.

A heavy heat settled low in her belly. "You're the one who took the sheets."

"As much as I'd like to call you on this bluff—"

"No bluff."

"We're already late. Put on a swimsuit, grab a wrap and a towel and meet me outside in fifteen minutes."

"Where are you going?"

His hot gaze scorched across her skin again. "Out, before I say to hell with it and climb back into that bed with you."

"I wouldn't mind."

"You would if you knew what we were doing."

Colt didn't exactly disappear. Instead, they managed to get ready together with only one or two brief delays when they got too close to each other and good intentions were overwhelmed.

He made a fruitless attempt to cover her eyes—Lena patently refusing to submit. They walked to the opposite side of the resort, Lena becoming more and more confused when they passed the pool, the beach and even the main hotel building. They were on the path toward the dock before realization struck.

"We're taking a boat ride?"

Colt answered, "Maybe." Although when they rounded the corner in the path it became obvious they were.

The boat—although she hated to use that term since it appeared big enough to carry twenty people—bobbed softly on the swells of a calm sea. A man, she assumed the captain, lounged against the tall wooden post the bow was tied off to.

"Welcome," the man said as he took Lena's hand and helped her aboard.

Once they were on, the captain went to the helm, which sat high above the deck. Beneath it, there was an open doorway and a set of stairs leading down into a dark, pleasant hold. Lena peeked far enough inside to see a small galley, table and banquette, and in the back, a wide bunk built straight into the side of the ship.

Spread across the surface of the table were several masks, fins and bent rubber tubes. Lena had never been snorkeling before, but she'd seen pictures of the equipment.

"We're going snorkeling?" she asked, spinning on her heel and ramming straight into Colt's chest.

His arms automatically wrapped around her, pulling her tight against his body.

"You said you wanted to go."

She'd made the comment once in passing, and he'd remembered. Reaching up on tiptoe she placed a quick kiss to the underside of his jaw. "This is very sweet."

He leered at her in an exaggerated gesture that made her smile widen. "I'm sure we can come up with a way for you to repay me."

Smacking him playfully, Lena twisted out of his hold and headed straight for the table. "Okay, so explain to me how all this works."

Lena was glad that she didn't get seasick as the boat bounced over the waves. After a few minutes below deck, they brought everything above, settling into the seats at the bow so that they could look out. Dolphins joined them, jumping playfully alongside the boat, keeping pace as they raced into open water.

The water was crystal clear and she was actually getting excited about the prospect of snorkeling. The captain explained that they were heading out to a sunken ship he promised would be teeming with a rainbow of fish. She had to admit that Colt's surprise was a good one. Touching in a way that made her heart constrict and race all at the same time.

This was the sort of thing a man did for his lover. And she could get used to being spoiled. The problem was it wasn't real. This experience, this week—they weren't real. She tried to keep reminding herself of that, but it was becoming harder and harder to do.

She had no idea what was going to happen at the end of the week. Whenever she let herself think about it, a sharp pain shot through the center of her chest.

But she refused to let her worry about tomorrow ruin today.

The boat powered down and the captain released the hydraulic anchor. Once they were secured and the only thing visible for miles around, the captain switched modes and became their snorkeling guide.

Colt, obviously comfortable around the equipment, sat silently and listened to the instructions their guide provided. They went over safety and signals. After practicing a couple of times on deck, she and Colt dove off a platform at the back of the boat and into the water. Their guide remained with the boat.

It took Lena a couple of tries to get the hang of diving beneath the surface without choking on the water that poured into her open breathing tube. But it didn't take long before she was cruising after Colt, who raced back and forth as if he were born with fins and gills. She knew that he was certified in scuba, but she was amazed by how natural he seemed in the water.

The sunken ship was nothing like she'd expected, nothing like the *National Geographic* specials she'd seen. The dark pieces of wood were hard to distinguish, covered in centuries of barnacles, sand and underwater debris. Once Colt pointed out what she was looking at, it became easier to distinguish the edges of the broken ship from the rock and reef around it.

It was cool to think that she was looking at a piece of history. However, it was a little creepy, as well, and she quickly abandoned the site to follow a school of brightly colored fish as they swam close to the surface.

She should have signaled that she was going up, but she knew Colt would have insisted he follow her. He was enjoying his exploration of the ship and she didn't want to ruin his experience. It just wasn't her thing.

Lena went up to clear her snorkel and simply floated with her face in the water staring at the vista below. It was easier up here—she could breathe regularly, and didn't have to worry about swallowing a mouthful of water. She could still see the pink, blue, green and yellow fish as they swam in and out of the ship and reef below.

She kept Colt in sight, watching as he moved down, over and through the ghostly timbers of the ship. He was beautiful, a sleek bullet cutting through the water, coming up for air every couple minutes.

She had no idea how long she stayed there. Her back, no longer covered by the water began to heat, but she didn't move. It actually felt good, a nice contrast to the cool water. Fifteen, twenty minutes later, Colt came barreling around the distant corner of the ship, heading straight for the surface. And her.

His gaze locked with hers through the wavy plastic of their masks. For a moment she thought she saw panic but as he got closer she convinced herself that she must have been wrong because all she saw in his clear green eyes was desire.

He shot through the surface of the water beside her, spraying droplets across her hot back. She lifted her face out of the water just as he reached for her and pulled her into his arms.

His snorkel dangled beside his face, caught in place by the connecting strap on the mask he'd shoved to the top of his head. Lena pushed up her mask as well, spitting out the bulky mouthpiece so that she could smile at him.

"Where did you go?" he asked.

His arms were cool as they touched her sun-warmed shoulders. She shrugged. "I like it better on the surface."

"I wish you'd told me you weren't enjoying this."

"Who said I wasn't? I like snorkeling just fine. I'm just not as experienced at it as you. You were having fun." She leaned closer into his embrace, mock-whispering as if she didn't want anyone around them to hear. "Besides, I enjoyed watching you."

Colt laughed. His teeth flashed in the sun and an answering bubble of happiness grew inside her.

The day was perfect. His arms were around her, his smooth skin sliding against hers. He didn't kiss her or caress her or turn up the dial on the desire that constantly simmered beneath the surface whenever they were together now.

Instead, he simply held her close as they bobbed together in the waves, enjoying the pleasure of the shared moment. Lena realized these stolen hours were the best of both worlds. The ease of their friendship had somehow melded with the passion they'd found.

And that bubble burst as she realized she loved him.

It slammed into her with enough force for her to lose her breath. No, no, no. How could she have let this happen? She wasn't supposed to fall for him.

Her legs jerked up in the water, her body curling around itself and the pain and fear rippling inside her.

"Are you okay?" Colt asked, his eyes, just moments ago glittering with the excitement of discovery, were now cloudy with worry.

Somewhere Lena found the strength to nod and give him a sickly smile that she knew was nowhere close to normal. But it was the best she could manage right now.

"I think I have a cramp." Lena reached down for her calf, rubbing the phantom pain.

What was she going to do? She'd promised him this would be no strings attached. She'd promised herself she wouldn't allow emotions and hormones to rule her decisions.

And, really, that was still possible. So she loved him. Hadn't she always? Sure, the emotion had somehow grown and changed, but she could deal with that.

At the end of the week, he would leave and head for whatever adventure came next. She'd go home, start circulating her résumé and try to find another steady, stable job as a graphic designer. Her skills were in high demand. And a few months from now, out of the blue, he would call.

And by then, maybe, she'd have figured out a way to deal with the inevitable pain.

Why had she fallen for Colt? The worst possible man for her to want. A nomad of the highest order, who didn't even bother ordering cable because he wasn't home long enough to watch it.

He was her opposite in every possible way. The craziest thing she'd ever done was deciding to buy her apartment even though she only had ten percent instead of the recommended twenty saved. He threw his body off the side of mountains, trekked into distant jungles, experienced exotic cultures. And enjoyed every second of it.

They would be terrible for each other. She couldn't ask him to give up that part of his life—his career, his dreams, the very fabric of his identity—anymore than she could change who she was and what she needed.

Dammit, she wanted to scream.

Somehow she managed to get back into the boat, although she didn't remember doing it. Colt insisted they eat lunch in the galley, to keep her pale skin out of the sun as much as possible. The dark, cool interior was far better than the bright sunlight outside. Beneath the stark sunshine, he might have seen more than she wanted him to.

She tried to recapture the enjoyment of the day, but couldn't seem to do it. At one point Colt suggested they head back, but that only added guilt to the mix she was struggling against. He'd gone to so much trouble to make her happy…even if it could only be for this one day.

Finally, the captain came down and said, "It's time

to start heading in. Marcy told me to have you back at two on the nose."

Together, they went to sit at the bow again. Lena curled her legs up onto the cushion beside her. Draping an arm around her shoulders, Colt pulled her closer against his body and leaned down to capture her lips.

The kiss was hot, as they all were with Colt, but there was a softness beneath it as well. Tears she desperately wanted to hold in stung the backs of her eyes. She let her eyelids slide shut to hide them.

She wanted the heat they'd shared the night before. She wanted to be consumed so that she could forget, for a little while anyway, what was eventually going to come.

Well, she supposed, there was one bright spot. Unlike when her mother had been overwhelmed by disappointment and despair, there was no one else in her life to be caught in the crosshairs of her devastation.

No, Lena clamped down hard on the inside of her cheek, ignoring the metallic tang of blood as it welled into her mouth. She refused to be that person. No matter what happened, she would not let this crush her.

When it was over, she'd tell Colt goodbye. And go on with the rest of her life. And find exactly what she was looking for.

If she could figure out what that was anymore.

THEY HAD JUST ENOUGH TIME to shower, change and get ready for Marcy's next assignment—a ballroom-dancing lesson followed by a party so that everyone could practice their newfound skills.

Lena was beautiful, as always. She'd dressed in a black strapless sheath that hugged her body and made his mouth water. She'd taken the time to pile her hair high on her head, mahogany curls cascading down to brush against the nape of her neck. Colt's fingers itched to sweep them away, to palm the curve of her neck and kiss her senseless.

He resisted, barely.

She'd been out of sorts since they'd gotten back into the boat this afternoon. He couldn't pinpoint what was wrong, but something definitely was. He'd asked, but she'd given him a quick—too quick—answer that she was fine.

He didn't believe her.

Perhaps his surprise hadn't been such a good idea after all. When they'd first reached the boat, she'd seemed excited. Even in the water, she'd been laughing and smiling, enjoying herself.

Now she was silent and distant. And he wasn't used to that. Aside from the details of her childhood, he was under the impression that they'd shared everything. In the past, he would have teased her until the truth spilled out. But this wasn't the past and the dynamic of their relationship had changed.

He no longer knew how to handle her. He was terrible at relationships, which was one reason he tried desperately not to have them. They were work. He had to consider someone else's feelings, wants and needs.

No woman had ever been important enough to deal with that headache. The difference was, with Lena, it didn't feel like a headache. He was genuinely worried about her. If she was upset, he wanted to help.

But he couldn't force her to talk to him.

They walked across the complex, entering the main resort building for the first time since checking in. A friendly girl greeted them, directing them up two floors to the ballroom at the end of the hallway.

Walking into the room, Colt had the sudden feeling that he'd stepped back in time a couple hundred years. The space was huge.

Floor-to-ceiling windows ran the entire length of one side, interspersed with French doors that led onto a full-length balcony. Through the glass Colt could see the scrolling ironwork that ringed the space. It looked as original to the structure as the hardwood floors, crystal chandeliers and period wall sconces.

Ornately framed artwork graced the walls. Depictions of scenes from Victorian ballrooms echoed what the current residents must have assumed took place inside the ballroom. Touches of the modern—Mikhail's light poles, a large rolling cart with sound equipment and the updated wiring that allowed for electrical lights—left him with a sort of distorted reality.

A small group of people were gathered at the far end of the room. Probably twenty or thirty total. There were two or three older couples, perhaps empty nesters enjoying their newfound freedom. The way they joked with each other, laughing and teasing, twisted something sharp inside him.

They reminded him of his parents. Before the accident his father had just retired, selling the business he'd spent all of his life building. His parents wouldn't get to enjoy those quiet years together and that made him sad.

Even now, years later, the pain of losing them was still so sharp. It would surprise him sometimes, coming out of nowhere, regret and loss tightening an ever-present band across his chest. Maybe if their deaths hadn't been so sudden, or if he hadn't lost them both at once. But Colt didn't think that would matter. He missed his mother's indulgent smile and his father's high expectations, and he always would. Losing them was the most difficult thing he'd ever had to deal with. And he never wanted to experience that kind of grief again.

Colt was locked somewhere inside the demons of his own past when a squeal shattered the moment.

Separating from the group, Georgie rushed up beside them, wrapping her arms around Lena and giving her a big hug. It didn't seem to register with her that Lena did little more than pat her on the back before trying to extricate herself from the other woman's grasp.

"What have y'all been up to since yesterday?" Georgie asked with a sly wink and a big white smile.

"Snorkeling," Lena said, looking around her, probably for the emergency exit.

Before she could find it, Marcy and Mikhail entered the room, followed by a striking couple who seemed to glide across the floor with effortless grace.

Marcy stopped in front of the gathered group. Putting on her straightest Manager smile, she said, "We're all excited to welcome you to our couples' ballroom class. I hope you're enjoying your stay at Escape. Please let us know if there's anything we can do to enhance your experience. Everyone enjoy the class."

The man stepped forward, his eyes running expertly over the crowd. "I'm Tony and this is my partner Sara. Our only rule is that everyone must have fun tonight. Does anyone have a request for which dance we learn?"

Behind them, Georgie's light, lyrical voice shouted, "The Lambda." Everyone chuckled at her mispronunciation of *Lambada*. Wesley groaned, but as Colt turned around to look at him, he noticed the man's arms were wrapped tightly around his wife.

Tony said, "Maybe we should start with something a little easier. How about the Tango?"

A general sound of acceptance rose from the group.

Marcy stepped up beside Tony and addressed everyone again. "Mikhail is going to be photographing one of our couples." She pointed toward them. Lena squirmed beside Colt as every eye in the place turned to take them in. "You might have seen them around the resort this week. They're going to be featured in an upcoming ad campaign and magazine spread. Mikhail's going to attempt to keep everyone else out of the shots because we value our guests' privacy. Rest assured we will be obtaining your permission if you appear in any of the photographs. In the meantime, just pretend that he isn't here."

Colt knew from experience that that was easier said than done. There was nothing like a camera to make the shyest person outgoing and the most flamboyant person retiring. People seemed to change, although now that he stopped to think about it, Lena hadn't.

With a clap, Tony and Sara began the class. Colt, who'd taken ballroom lessons as a child, immediately picked up the hold that he remembered. Lena, on the other hand, turned out to have two left feet. He honestly never would have guessed it. She was fluid and sensual in bed. But on the dance floor, her arms and legs moved as if her knees and elbows had been frozen in place.

"Lena, can you look a little more…relaxed?" Mikhail asked as he spun around them.

She grimaced. "I don't think so."

Mikhail sighed and dropped to his knees, setting up for an elongated shot that would minimize her stiffness in the final product. Colt admired the man's adaptability.

Georgie and Wesley wedged their way beside them. The two were obviously no strangers to a ballroom floor. Colt would wager she'd insisted on six months of classes before the wedding. He wondered, as practical and detail-oriented as Lena was why she hadn't done the same.

"Didn't you and Wyn take lessons for your first dance?" he asked, forcing her backward in the basic step.

"No. We weren't going to have a traditional first dance."

"I bet that went over well with Diane."

Lena stumbled, unable to keep up with the advancing steps of the dance. Colt caught her, deliberately slowing their pace.

"She didn't know," she gritted out through stiff lips.

Sara walked up behind Lena. Without any warning, she bracketed her hands over Lena's hips, making her jump in surprise.

"It's all in the hips, Lena. Loosen up and just let yourself feel the beat of the music. Slow, slow, quick, quick, slow."

Colt wanted to yell at everyone to leave her alone, but he realized that wouldn't solve anything. He was about to whisk her away, photographs and party be damned, but before he could do it, Georgie and Wesley slid to a smooth stop beside them.

Wesley had his wife bent over backward, supporting her with a lunging knee and his strong frame. Georgie's head was thrown back, her spine arched, her blond hair trailing against the floor.

Hanging upside down, Georgie looked straight at Lena and said, "Honey, it's like sex standing up. Colt, however did you get through the reception?"

He could see it coming. Colt watched as anger, frustration and something akin to pain gathered deep in Lena's blue-gray eyes. They darkened and swirled, and even he was powerless to stop the explosion.

"We did not have a reception. We did not have a wedding. We are not married!" Lena yelled, her voice getting louder with each statement, until the entire room was staring.

11

THE MOMENT THE WORDS LEFT Lena's mouth she regretted them. Georgie was speechless, something she was certain hadn't happened often in the young woman's life. Wesley pulled her slowly up out of their dip, sheltering her with his arms and body. A shocked, hurt expression filled Georgie's face. For a minute, Lena felt as if she'd just kicked a puppy. A sickly sensation that she didn't like settled thick in the bottom of her stomach.

A rather large scowl pinched Marcy's mouth. And Colt simply watched Lena, as if trying to decide what she might do next so he could formulate a plan of action.

Reaching up, Lena rubbed both hands into her eye sockets, hoping that the pressure would relieve the headache she'd been fighting all day.

It didn't work.

Colt tried to pull her into the protection of his arms, too, but she wouldn't let him. Instead, she turned to Georgie and said, "I'm sorry. I shouldn't have taken my frustration out on you."

And then she turned around and walked away.

Lena could hear the hushed murmurs as the group behind her began to discuss her outburst. She hated that, knowing she'd let her emotions get the best of her and made herself a spectacle.

It was exactly what she always tried to avoid, and the unwanted attention reminded her painfully of her wedding day.

She was so close to the edge. Volatile and unpredictable. Her entire body was overrun by chaos, and she didn't like it.

She didn't want to go back to the bungalow. It wouldn't take long for Colt to follow her and he'd want to talk about what was wrong. And she couldn't explain it…not to him. Not this time.

And that made things worse. Colt was the person she'd always turned to for help, for advice. He might have been worlds away, but she could always count on him when she truly needed someone.

This time, she didn't have that. She longed for the easiness of their friendship, the comfortable familiarity they'd always shared. It was definitely gone, overrun by her own complicated emotions and uncertainty. Lena feared they'd never find that ease again.

A blast of music ricocheted off the buildings around her. Laughter and happiness underlined the sound and right now, that was exactly what she was looking for. Something to take her mind off of everything that was going wrong.

Heading in the general direction of the noise, Lena rounded the corner in a path she hadn't been down all week and discovered a brightly lit bar. It only had three and a half walls, the center of one wall standing open to the night so guests could wander in from the beach. The thatching from the roof blew in the gentle breeze, making a rustling sound that could barely be heard above the jovial voices.

She walked inside and immediately realized she'd stumbled onto the singles' side of the resort.

Women and men were bumping and grinding on the dance floor in the center of the room. The smell of expectation and sex seemed to linger everywhere. It was clearly a pickup place.

And while she didn't feel completely right taking a seat at the bar, she realized she probably belonged here much more than she had at the ballroom party she'd just ditched. She *was* single, after all. And she supposed it was time she got used to the idea.

Although, she certainly didn't feel single. In fact, she had no interest in any of the men in the place. And there were some her single friends would definitely have drooled over.

"What can I get you?" the bartender asked. He was already pouring another drink, even as he leaned forward to hear her.

"I don't care. Something strong and sweet."

Lena downed two of the orange-and-yellow concoctions he brought her in quick succession. Her gaze swept across the crowd. Not one of the men had approached her since she'd sat down. She wasn't sure whether to be relieved or insulted.

Before she had a chance to decide, Colt slid up to the bar beside her.

"How did you find me?" she asked, without bothering to look at him.

She didn't need to. Her body had begun reacting the second he walked through the door. Her heart stuttered inside her chest and her body began to heat like an engine sitting idle waiting for the expert hand of its driver.

Damn, she thought.

That was why none of the men here mattered, because they weren't Colt.

"Process of elimination."

She looked at him from beneath her lashes as he sat down beside her. "Surely you didn't check every single building."

"Why not? You're upset and I'm your friend."

Four days ago, that would have been enough for her. But Lena feared it wasn't anymore. She no longer wanted Colt to be her friend—or *just* her friend—she wanted him to love her.

And he didn't. Oh, he cared about her or he wouldn't be sitting there beside her. But it wasn't the same. And it wasn't enough.

"I could tell all day something was off. Want to talk about it?"

No, she didn't. What she wanted to do was have another drink, to bump and grind with him on the dance floor and then make mad, passionate love with him all night.

Instead, she said, "I think it's just all finally hitting me."

"What, that you never loved Wyn?"

Lena wanted to laugh. If he'd said that to her days ago she would have vehemently denied it. In fact, she thought maybe she had. She would have argued that they'd had a perfectly good relationship, even if it hadn't been filled with passion. However, that was before she knew what real love felt like.

It hurt. It made you vulnerable. It was bliss and fear all wrapped up together.

"No, I didn't love Wyn."

"So why were you going to marry him?"

"Because he was there. Because he was good and decent—or at least I thought so at the time. Because we could have had a perfectly satisfying life."

"You mean boring."

"I mean normal. We would have bought a house together. Had a couple of kids. Chaired the PTA and sat on the bleachers together at T-ball games."

Colt spun the bottom of his glass around and around between his hands. Lena's gaze was drawn, to their strength, the single scar that ran diagonally from the corner of his thumb up over his wrist.

"And that's what you want," he finally said.

She stared down into the bottom of her own glass. The frozen concoction had melted, the yellow and orange mingling together. The drink had looked bright and happy before. Now it just looked sad.

Without realizing what she was doing, Lena opened her mouth and told Colt the truth.

"I don't know what I want anymore. I'm so confused."

"Do you have to decide tonight? Who said you had to have all of the answers all of the time?"

"But I hate being…directionless. I hate not knowing where I'm going and how I'm going to get there. I like being in control."

Colt smiled, a sort of sad twist of his lips. "I know, but life doesn't always work that way. If there's one thing I've learned traveling the world and seeing different cultures it's that life throws you curveballs. You show your character through how you deal with them."

Character. She didn't even know what that meant anymore. She'd dealt with plenty of curveballs in her life. By herself. She was tired and wondered when it would be enough.

She realized Colt was just trying to help. And the things he'd dealt with made her issues seem somehow petty in comparison. Unfortunately, he was part of the problem, and his inability to realize that made the entire conversation a little difficult. Rather than have it go in a direction she didn't want to deal with, she decided to lighten the mood.

"Great pep talk, Yoda," she groused, leaning her body into his and knocking him sideways on the stool.

"Hey." He pushed back. "I'm wise beyond my years and you should listen to me."

"Please. If I did that you'd have talked me into jumping out of an airplane so that I could prove to myself I have the strength to get through this."

"Don't knock the power of the adrenaline rush until

you've tried it. Besides, there's something about facing fear head-on that reminds us we can handle more than we think."

"I am not going skydiving. I don't care what argument you use."

They sat together in silence for several minutes, lost in their own thoughts.

Lena realized that on some level Colt was right. She'd deal with the aftermath of Wyn's betrayal because she had to. And maybe knowing she'd never really loved him would make it easier in the end.

"If I can't convince you to skydive, can I at least persuade you to come to bed?"

And she'd handle their parting, as well. Because she had to—there was no other choice. But in the meantime, she had two days left to enjoy. And there was no reason not to make the most of them.

"I'm sure something can be arranged," she said, sliding off her stool. Anticipation buzzed through her blood. It was always there, just beneath the surface, waiting.

Colt followed her as they weaved through the undulating bodies and steamy heat of the bar. She threw a teasing glance behind her and relished the way his eyes sharpened.

She managed to keep people and tables between them so that he was several steps behind as she reached the beach exit. The minute she stepped outside, she broke into a sprint.

Calling behind her, she taunted, "But you'll have to catch me first."

COLT CAUGHT HER halfway down the path. He spun her in his arms, his mouth was rough as it claimed hers, but she met him thrust for thrust. They rushed together, groping mouths and urgent fingers.

His thigh wedged between hers and the exquisite bolt of awareness that rocketed through her sex almost sent her to her knees. His commanding hold on her was intoxicating. Every step he took forward drove her relentlessly back toward their bungalow and the rising passion building inside her. That passion was quickly becoming the easiest thing between them.

She couldn't help but be aware that their retreat echoed that of the dance she'd sorely butchered. Out here, alone with him, it was effortless. She didn't have to think, to worry that she was doing the wrong thing. Even without music, her body undulated against him, eager to go wherever he might lead. Inside, surrounded by people, she'd been stiff and uncomfortable and she knew it had shown.

But she hadn't known how to fix it.

"See, you *can* dance," he whispered against her ear, pulling her chest flush against him. "You just have to let yourself feel."

Maybe it was the dark night or the drinks she'd consumed, but she found herself saying, "I can't. I don't trust it. The pulse deep inside my muscles that urges me to just let go." That thing deep inside that insisted she should take a chance and stop fighting what she really wanted. "It's overwhelming. I'm afraid to lose myself."

"Do you trust me?" he asked.

Lena pulled back. She knew in her head that the question was simple. The answer, however, was not.

"With my body? Absolutely."

Apparently he was satisfied with her answer—they burst through the bungalow door. With a well-placed kick, Colt closed it behind them.

He moved her across the floor in the mimicked steps of the dance until the backs of her knees struck the edge of the bed. She toppled over, not even trying to keep her balance. She sprawled before him.

He towered above her, staring down with those intense, watchful, all-seeing eyes. He knew her too well and she wondered if he'd caught her equivocation after all.

Lena fell back on her elbows. His knee joined her on the bed, dipping the mattress next to her hip and rolling her body against him. Her mouth was suddenly dry. She tried to swallow but nothing was there.

Somehow this moment felt more important. It wasn't the first capitulation to a startling new awareness. It wasn't a hurried tumble on the ground because they'd both been scared and worried and needed the feel of each other. Nor was it the perfectly prepared seduction complete with romantic setting.

What it was, was emotional, more so than Lena wanted. There was a connection, an understanding, that hadn't been there before. She wondered if the difference was in her, the acknowledgment of her true feelings. Or was it part of him, too?

Lena realized it was the first time they'd actually had sex in a bed. The first night had been awkward, the second she'd been alone. Then they'd been out in the cave and finally inside the tent. Anytime they'd fallen into the bed, it had been from exhaustion that immediately claimed them both.

Maybe that was the difference.

He overwhelmed her as he always did. He tugged his shirt off over his head. Lena reached for him, running her fingers across the ridge of his pecks and abs. His skin was damp.

She arched beneath him, wanting to rub against him like a languid cat. He took the opportunity to tug at the zipper that ran along the line of her body, his fingers tickling against the swell of her breast and sliding over her skin to the curve of her hip. When he reached the zipper's end, he peeled the fabric away.

Her panties and bra joined the rest. Colt was braced above her. She marveled at the strength of his arms, the ripple of muscles, as he levered himself away. She wanted him to give in and fall onto her waiting body. She wanted to feel him, all of him, against her.

Hooking her feet around his ankles, she jerked his legs out from under him. He collapsed with a whoosh of surprise on top of her.

"Why did you do that?"

Lena undulated her hips beneath him, grinding his erection against her stomach. "So I could do that."

Grasping her hips, Colt rolled them both, reversing their positions and settling her sex over his erection.

"Do that again," he ordered. She complied, sending a bolt of need straight through her body as she moved her hips against him.

"Holy sh..." His words trailed off as his eyes closed, an expression of pure rapture crossing his face. She did it again just to see that all-consuming pleasure. She relished knowing she wasn't the only one overwhelmed by what was happening.

His eyes opened again, glittering at her with an intense hunger she felt down to her bones. Rearing up from beneath her, he covered her aching breasts with his hands. Her nipples spiked against his palms. He rubbed them in circles, soothing the throbbing before teasing them into hungry peaks again.

His head dipped as he sucked one deep into his mouth. Wet heat surrounded her. Her hips jerked against him, searching for more. Her fingers fisted into the hair at the nape of his neck, holding him where she wanted him.

Lena threw her head back, exposing her throat. The world spun around her. It took her a second to realize the motion was real and not just her equilibrium being bombarded with sensations. Her back bounced softly on the bed before settling. Her feet dangled off, forgotten and unnecessary.

His mouth trailed kisses across her stomach; his fingers found the slick heat of her sex and dove inside. The invasion was sudden and shocking, but Lena wanted it so badly that she didn't care. In fact, her hips immediately tried to push him into a faster rhythm so she could find relief from the storm building inside her.

But he wouldn't let her off that easily.

He brought her to the brink of orgasm so many times she lost count. His hand. His mouth. She was sobbing, her useless fingers scrabbling against his shoulders, trying to find purchase, anything that would compel him to give her the relief she needed.

She tried to reach for him, to fill her hands with the heat of his erection, but he stopped her. Undeterred, she found other ways. The arch of her foot brushed slowly against the jutting length of his cock. He gasped and then growled. She used her calf, her knee and inner edge of her thigh.

With soft pressure, she used his own body against him, sandwiching his cock between them. The pressure of her slipping back and forth against him drove them both insane. But it still wasn't enough.

She wanted to feel him, to hold him, to taste him. To torture him half as much as he was torturing her. With the last of her strength, Lena grasped his face. Looking him in the eye, she begged, "Colt, please."

His eyes were hot, his face drawn hard by the desire whipping through both of them. He was as close to the edge as she was. Maybe closer. Lena never realized how sexy it was to have a man so enthralled with her that her pleasure made him delirious. It was intoxicating.

Colt pushed against her hold. Lena collapsed to the bed, her thighs wet with her own desire, open and sprawled. He could do anything he wanted to her and she knew she'd love every second of it.

He paused only long enough to grab the condom—not something they'd forgotten since the cave.

His knees nudged her legs open wider. Her internal muscles contracted, sensing they'd soon be filled with him. He claimed her mouth, breathing her name across her lips before he did. His tongue slipped between her lips as his sex slid home inch by inch. Her body stretched, taking him in and holding him.

Her muscles quivered against the slow pace he was setting. She wanted him to rush, to finish it, but he wouldn't. Instead, he grasped both of her hands, threaded their fingers together and locked them beside her head.

Her body arched beneath him so that the swollen tips of her breasts brushed against his chest with each deliberate thrust. He stared down at her, his gaze deep and powerful.

A swell of something so overwhelming burst deep inside. She felt vulnerable, caught there beneath him, open, delirious with passion. It was too much. This was too much.

To protect herself, Lena let her eyes slip shut.

But Colt wasn't having it. With a growling demand, he said, "Look at me."

And she was powerless to resist.

She saw more than she wanted. Revealed more than she'd meant to give. In that moment there were no barriers between them. Not her fear nor their past. Not the uncertainty of what might come nor the understanding that it wouldn't be enough.

It was just them, connected in a timeless act that united them in a way that nothing else could.

Colt thrust against her. Her breath caught as he hit the sweet spot inside. Her hips rushed to meet him. Deliberately, he drove them both to the edge, meeting and grinding and demanding more. She wanted it to go on forever, to be so completely lost in the moment that it never ended.

But that couldn't happen.

Little bursts of electricity tingled up her spine. Her sex quivered. Colt yelled her name, surging deep inside her. Every part of her lost control, surrendering to the power of the connection building between them.

12

COLT WOKE SLOWLY. He felt almost hungover, although he hadn't had enough to drink for that to be the case. Beside him, Lena was buried beneath the covers, the soft contours of her body snuggled against him.

Last night had been intense. More intimate than anything he'd ever experienced before. He'd had plenty of sex in his life, but nothing came close to comparing.

His desire for Lena was intoxicating. Not just the sexual interludes, but the moments in between. Listening to her laugh. Watching her excitement as she learned something new. Even the way they disagreed made him want her more.

She challenged him in a way that no other woman ever had.

They had two days left, and looking down at the soft glow of Lena's skin, he realized it wasn't going to be nearly enough.

Unfortunately, he had no idea how to convince her of that.

The timing surely sucked. Less than a week ago

she'd been standing at an altar ready to marry a different man. But even she admitted that had been a mistake. She'd never loved Wyn.

The question was could she ever love Colt?

Fear roiled deep in his belly. It suffused his body with a restless heat that had him kicking off the covers and pacing away from her and the bed they'd shared.

He wasn't ready for this. He wasn't ready to love Lena.

She stirred restlessly in the bed, making little protesting noises as she rolled into the imprint of where he'd just been. Letting out a sigh, she burrowed deeper, apparently satisfied with the spot that she'd found.

There was the real possibility that he might lose her. Not just the new physical side to their relationship, but the friendship they'd built across distance and years.

Colt fought the urge to rip her out of the comfort of the covers and make her promise that she'd never leave him alone. Doing that wouldn't help.

Tight on the heels of that first inclination came another. The urge to love her completely, to brand her as his in every way possible, rose up inside him. Needing some air and distance before he did something stupid, Colt threw on the first thing he came to—a worn pair of jeans—and headed out onto their private patio.

The soft blue water in their infinity pool shimmered and mocked him. They hadn't even bothered to take advantage of it, which was a shame. Maybe later, when he had his emotions in check, they could swim together. Preferably naked.

He walked around to the far side of the pool. From

that vantage point, he could see the edge of the sea in the distance. The jungle, untamed as ever, was off to his left. He stood there, staring out into the unruly beauty.

A loud ringing interrupted the silence. It took him several seconds to realize it was coming from inside the bungalow. His cell phone.

He'd almost forgotten its existence over the past several days. Racing back inside, Colt scrambled to answer it before it could disturb Lena.

"Hello," he said in a hushed tone, moving back outside.

"Colt? Is that you?" The connection was awful, loud crackling interspersed with a low hum. He should probably know who it was, but with all of the interference he didn't.

"Who else would be answering my cell? Who's this?"

"Desmond Owens with the production team in Peru."

A drumbeat picked up somewhere in his chest.

"Desmond. How's the shoot?"

"Not…great." Desmond's response crackled. "Several of the crew came down with dengue fever. The local doctors say they won't be ready to return to the field for at least two weeks. And yesterday Ryan—" the man Desmond had hired as director instead of Colt "—fell off a cliff. He's going to be fine, but he broke a leg and dislocated his shoulder. They medevaced him to the closest hospital."

"That's awful. I'm sorry you guys are having so much trouble. But I'm in the middle of the Caribbean. What can I do from here?"

"We've put the project on hold for a few days. It sets us way behind schedule and plays hell with our budget, but I just don't have another choice. I was hoping that would be enough time for you to get here."

"Get there?"

"I need you to direct."

"Direct?" Shock, excitement and a rush of adrenaline shot through his body.

This was the chance he'd been waiting for. The break he needed to prove himself. The Peru shoot was complicated. It covered an archaeological find that was set to rival that of Machu Picchu. But the film site was remote.

Just getting there involved hours on a plane, connecting multiple times. Then driving to a local village and hiking through the thick jungle to a spot that had been virtually untouched for hundreds of years. The crew had packed in all their equipment. Not to mention generators, since they'd be living and working out there for weeks.

It would be challenging, but that's what had excited Colt about the project in the first place.

"We'll work out all the details when you get here. I've already booked you a flight leaving St. Lucia this afternoon."

"Presumptuous, aren't you?"

"Desperate is more like it. I don't know anyone else who could step up and fill Ryan's shoes so well."

Colt ran his hand through his hair. The temptation was great. It was what he'd been working so hard for over the past several years.

A small sound made him whirl to find Lena standing behind him. She was framed by the doorway to the patio. Her hair was mussed, her skin still flushed from sleep. She'd thrown on a shirt that barely skimmed the tops of her thighs. She looked rumpled and sleepy.

Everything except her eyes—they were wide awake. Watchful. Somewhat wary.

"Let me get back to you."

"But we don't—" Desmond protested.

Colt cut him off. "I'll call you back in twenty minutes," he said, hanging up.

The cell sat heavy in his hand, as if it suddenly carried more gravitational pull than the rest of the world around them. And in some way, Colt supposed it did. It was the connection to everything he'd ever wanted. Five days ago he wouldn't even have hesitated.

Now he looked across the infinity pool standing between him and Lena and wondered if the space had somehow gotten bigger.

"I'm so happy for you, Colt. You deserve this job. You've worked hard for a chance like this."

He nodded.

It felt as if he had a choice. As if he had to decide between taking the job that he'd been waiting for all his life and staying with the woman that he loved. But that wasn't right.

Why could he only have one or the other? Wasn't there a way to have both?

"Come with me," he said.

"What?" Her body rocked backward as if she'd been physically struck by his words.

"Come to Peru with me."

Colt watched as her eyes widened. She swallowed hard, her throat working overtime. A war of emotions crossed her face. They moved so fast that he couldn't determine what she was thinking.

He moved slowly around the pool, but stopped when she took a single step away.

Dread, hope and an engulfing grief that he recognized but didn't understand swamped him.

"Lena," he whispered, "come with me."

He knew her answer even before she said it, the reality dawning right along with the sadness that filled her eyes.

She shook her head.

"I can't."

"WHAT DO YOU MEAN YOU CAN'T? You have nothing to go home to. No fiancé, no job. What's holding you there, Lena? Come with me."

His words hurt. And they scared her senseless. There was nothing in D.C. to return for. Her job was gone. Even if Mr. Rand didn't fire her, she couldn't continue to work for the company. It wouldn't feel right, seeing Wyn and his father every day.

Her relationship was dead. The life she'd imagined had disappeared before it'd even had a chance to start. Unpacking the boxes in her apartment was really the only thing she had to look forward to.

How pathetic was that?

But what Colt offered wasn't any better. In fact, it was worse.

"And what exactly would I do in Peru? Wash your clothes? Cook your meals? Or would my only responsibility be to make myself available whenever you weren't busy and wanted a roll in the hay?"

Colt's eyes narrowed. "Don't do this."

"Do what? Ask the hard questions?"

"Bring everything down to the lowest common denominator. Don't put a wedge between us."

She laughed, the sound ringing with bitterness. "Us? There is no us, Colt. There's now, this week. We both knew when it was over we'd go our separate ways. It's just going to happen a little earlier than we'd planned."

She shrugged, a sharp pain lancing through her chest. She resisted the urge to wrap her arms around herself, not wanting him to see her weakness.

"I will not follow you like some bitch in heat. I will not be my mother."

"What the hell does your mother have to do with this?" he bellowed, frustration and anger quickly overshadowing everything else.

"Nothing. I have a life. A job I enjoy. Pieces to pick up and put back together. My place is in D.C."

She would not leave everything behind without a backward glance for a man, not even for Colt. Part of her wanted to give in, to agree to anything he asked. It would be so easy to do.

But he hadn't offered her promises. He hadn't told her he loved her or needed her or wanted something more than an extension of the pleasure they'd found together on the island.

Maybe if he had…

But he hadn't and she refused to be ruled by her libido. With Wyn she'd had a relationship that was passionless but practical. And with Colt she'd had the all-consuming passion that clouded her brain and made her contemplate making bad decisions.

When would she find a happy medium? Someone who could give her everything she wanted and needed? Passion, happiness, a stable future and roots that ran so deep they couldn't be removed.

That's what she deserved. But at the moment, the idea of ever finding it felt foreign and unattainable.

Still, she refused to settle for something less. She refused to fall into the same trap her mother had. She refused to lose herself simply to please a man.

She refused to let the moment when Colt walked away break her.

As if realizing that his outburst hadn't helped his case any, Colt lowered his voice and quietly countered, "Everything will be there after Peru. You can deal with it all then."

"No, no, I can't. I can't put my life on hold because you're not ready to give up our vacation fling."

He reached for her, but Lena pulled away. If he touched her, she might cave. And then she'd never forgive herself.

"Go, Colt. I want you to. I know that this is the break you've been waiting for. I'm happy for you, really I am."

Colt's jaw tightened. His entire body was pulled tight. She knew he wanted to say more, wanted to come up with some argument that was sure to change her mind.

But there wasn't one. They didn't have a future. She

knew that. Better to end things now and minimize the pain as much as possible.

The loud ring of his cell blasted between them. Colt's hand tightened around it before pulling it up to look at the screen. He didn't immediately answer. Instead, he looked at her over the top of it and said again, "Come with me."

Lena swallowed, forcing back the lump of tears that was stuck in her throat. With a slow shake of her head, she said, "I can't."

Spinning away from her, Colt answered the call. She listened, unable to move away and save herself the heartache, as he did exactly what she'd told him to do and accepted Desmond's offer.

As she sagged against the frame of the door, the pain burst full-fledged through her body. *Finally* was all she could think. Here was the pain she'd come to expect.

It was over and some day she'd figure out how to deal with it. In the meantime, she refused to fall apart. No one would find her unwashed and unhappy, so weighted down by grief and pain that she couldn't get out of bed. Tissues would not lie crumpled between the layers of her bed. She would not refuse to eat for days and weeks. No one would watch her waste away, losing twenty pounds she couldn't afford in the space of a few days.

She would not let herself be held hostage by these emotions.

Instead, she sat quietly and watched as Colt went through the bungalow packing his bags. Within thirty minutes all evidence that he'd even been there had disappeared.

At the door, his hand wrapped tightly around the handle of his bag, Colt paused. He looked back at her across the intimate space they'd shared. He paused, staring at her for several seconds before finally saying, "I hope you'll be happy."

The door had barely closed before she gave in to the torrent of emotions rushing through her. Tears flowed down her face, silent and as lonely as she suddenly felt.

She'd made the right decision.

So why did it hurt so much?

13

STALKING INTO THE MAIN LOBBY, Colt headed for the receptionist's desk. There was one more thing he needed to do before he left.

"I need to see Marcy, please."

The woman behind the desk cringed away from him, letting him know that the expression on his face was probably not the best one to be wearing if he wanted to charm anyone into anything. He tried to wipe the scowl off his face, but it wouldn't seem to budge.

The woman backed away from the desk, glancing behind her to the hallway leading into the offices. "I'll go get her," she said reluctantly.

Colt was in no mood to wait.

Rounding the desk, he headed for the opening, beating her there.

"Wait, sir, you can't go in there." She tried to skirt in front of him. He'd give the tenacious little thing points for effort, despite the fact that he could have picked her up and moved her aside with nothing but his pinky finger.

"Trust me, Marcy won't mind if I find her."

"Trust me, she will," the woman answered dryly, but apparently she realized there wasn't much she could do to stop him.

Colt vaguely heard her pick up the phone and whisper into it as he disappeared into the back offices. He probably had less than five minutes before some security force came swooping down to save little Marcy. By then he knew she'd stop whoever tried to throw him out.

Sticking his head into several offices, he noticed that they were all neat, with mismatched furniture that somehow fit the homey, eclectic feel of the resort. Escape was no doubt a pleasant place to work. Although, at the moment Colt wasn't exactly harboring the warm and fuzzies for it.

A light shone out into the hallway from the last door on the right. It was early enough that he supposed no one else had made it in, but Marcy was here. Lucky for him.

Rounding the corner, he plopped down into her guest chair. Marcy did a double take, pulling her focus away from the computer screen that sat adjacent to the corner of her desk.

A scroll of color caught Colt's eye before she had a chance to minimize the screen. It was a photograph of Lena and himself.

"Colt. What are you doing here? I thought you'd be sleeping in today. We don't have anything scheduled until your couples massages later this afternoon."

"That's what I need to talk to you about." His harsh

voice had Marcy shifting in her chair, and glancing back at her computer screen, no doubt just to make sure the pictures weren't still revolving across it.

"Don't tell me you're one of those men who refuse to get a massage. You know, there's nothing sexual about it. I promise our staff is highly trained and extremely professional."

"I'm sure they are, but that's not the problem."

She frowned. "Then what is?"

"Something's come up and I have to leave."

She sputtered, at a loss for words for several seconds. Colt got the impression that rarely happened to Marcy. "But you can't. We haven't finished the sessions."

They had, although she wasn't ready to admit it yet. He'd only gotten a quick glimpse of the picture as it had flashed across her screen, but it had been enough to recognize good work. If he hadn't seen it, it might not have occurred to him to use the quality of what she already had as an argument against the need for more. But since he had…

"Show me." He gestured to the screen now displaying a generic beach scene.

"Show you what?" she asked.

"The photographs. I want to see them."

She studied him for several seconds. He assumed she was weighing her options and the potential consequences of doing as he asked. She made a move toward her screen but before she could touch it a man burst into the room. If Colt remembered right, this was the head of security they'd met the morning they came out of the jungle.

"Tina said there was a problem." The man skidded to a halt just inside the doorway. His eyes took in everything. Colt appreciated the thorough calculation used to assess the threat. No doubt he was former police or military.

"Everything's fine, Zane." Marcy gestured between the two men. "I can't remember if you two were introduced. Colt Douglas meet Zane Edwards, our head of security. Colt is part of the couple we're using for the ad campaign. He dropped by to discuss something with me."

"Tina said it was more like 'pushed in' than 'dropped by.'" The other man's eyes narrowed in consideration as they swept over Colt. He was happy that he was sitting down. Less chance Zane would consider him a threat. He was also pretty happy to notice the other man didn't have a gun tucked into a holster at his shoulder...unless he kept his beneath his black T-shirt and Colt just didn't see how the man could have hidden it.

Swiveling in his chair to face Zane, Colt decided some damage control couldn't hurt. "I apologize if I frightened Tina. I didn't mean to."

Zane harrumphed, but he let Colt's apology pass without really challenging it.

"Well, if you're certain everything's all right." Zane's eyes bored into Marcy's as if looking for some minute signal she might send.

"I promise she's not in any danger, at least from me. If you need a secret word or code or something go ahead and ask her for it. She isn't under duress."

"Honestly, Zane, I appreciate your concern but we're

fine. I'll call you if I need you," Marcy said, lifting up her cell phone from the desk where it had been lying beneath her computer monitor. "Anything else going on that I need to be aware of?"

"Not a thing," Zane said, already backing toward the door. The man's eyes swung to Colt's, his hazel gaze a bit unsettling. "I'll be keeping an eye on the hallway from the Crow's Nest."

It was clearly a warning, an unnecessary one, but he supposed he couldn't fault Zane for doing his job and doing it well. "Whatever makes you happy, man," Colt said with a shrug.

Turning on his heel, Zane disappeared almost as quickly and silently as he'd entered.

"I'm guessing he can kill with his bare hands," Colt quipped, returning his focus to Marcy.

"In many and varying ways. Part of me wishes I was daring enough to ask him for a demonstration."

"You haven't?"

"Are you kidding me? Did you see the size of his biceps? No, thank you."

Colt chuckled. Zane's appearance had managed to do one thing, if nothing else. It had defused the tension he'd carried with him into the room. He was angry and on edge, but that wasn't Marcy's fault.

"I really am sorry that I barged in here this way," he smiled at her.

She shook her head. "You truly can't help it, can you?"

"Help what?"

"That mischievous, impish charm thing that you've got going."

"I don't have a clue what you're talking about."

"I know. That's the problem." Reaching for her mouse, she started the slide show. "Here, let me show you."

His original intention was to glance through what they already had and use them to convince Marcy she had enough photographs. But the minute she flipped the screen toward him and the photos started scrolling that all changed. Photographs whizzed by, a kaleidoscope of memories from the past several days.

"Here," she said as the merry-go-round of colors stopped. A photograph from their first night at dinner popped up onto the screen. Lena was clearly uncomfortable. Her body and face were stiff and awkward.

He thought back to that night, after their first kiss. At the time he'd just assumed the whole photo-session thing was bothering her. In retrospect, he wondered if it had actually been residual awareness from their kiss that had her strung so tight.

The next photograph was of them on the beach. The tension was gone, replaced by the relaxed way her body leaned against his. Their heads were tilted together and for all intents and purposes they looked like a couple, one that shared the comfortable familiarity only achieved through time and common history.

Marcy scrolled through the photos again, flying past the rest of that evening to shots from the next day. By the pool they'd been laughing and relaxed. But there was more. Mikhail had managed to catch several candid shots. In one Lena was studying Colt beneath her lashes, stealing a glance while he wasn't looking. In another, he was devouring her with his eyes while she was focused on the pages of her book.

The sexual chemistry between them was almost palpable. Never in his life had he felt this exposed.

There was no doubt they were beautiful shots. Mikhail really was a talented photographer. If Colt had been looking at the final products through the filter of his education and experience he might have seen them in a different light.

But he couldn't separate that professional part of himself from the man who was staring at the woman he loved as she slowly moved closer and closer.

When they reached the group of photos from the night in the bungalow Colt felt heat suffuse his body. The first few obviously didn't work. But the rest were dripping with a sensuality that he didn't appreciate sharing with anyone. If he'd realized at the time, he would have kicked Mikhail out on his ass.

"Enough," he said, his voice rough and broken. He didn't want to see any more. It was too painful watching the progression of their affair knowing now how it would end.

There was one thing he knew for certain. No one could see these. They were too personal, too painful to share with the world. "You can't use those."

"Of course I can," Marcy said, her voice steady and self-assured.

"You don't understand. I can't let you use those photographs." He turned his gaze to hers. "I can't let the world see them."

"Why not? They're beautiful. The photographic evolution of a love affair."

"No, you don't understand. It's over. That's why I'm leaving."

"What?" Marcy shook her head as if hoping that some random piece would shake loose and what he'd just said would finally make sense. "What happened?"

He didn't answer, how could he when he wasn't entirely sure himself? Instead, he focused on the one problem he could solve. "I'll pay for the photographs. I'll pay for Mikhail's expenses and those of his crew. I'll pay for the week here at the resort and any extras that you arranged. I'll even pay for the new shoot you'll have to schedule to replace this one."

"But... No. I need these photographs in the next few weeks or we'll miss the deadline for the photo spread in *Worldwide Travel*."

"Then I'll pay for any rush fees required."

Marcy flopped back. The leather of her desk chair creaked with the force of her body. "What if I don't want to deal with the headache, Colt? Money can't solve everything."

"From my experience, money can solve everything. Everything except grief."

"Again, what if I refuse?"

"I'll get my lawyers involved."

"That won't do you much good. You signed an agreement."

"Maybe, but the court system is liable to issue an

injunction preventing you from using the photographs until everything is settled. That could take a while. Especially when you're dealing with multiple court systems that might have jurisdiction."

Marcy's eyes glittered and her jaw locked hard beneath her unsmiling mouth. "Where's the charm now, huh? Why are you doing this, Colt?"

"Because I can't stand the idea of her seeing those photographs and figuring out just how vulnerable I am."

"Men!" Marcy exclaimed, throwing her hands up into the air. "Would that be so damn bad?"

"I asked her to come with me." His eyes found Marcy's. He had no idea why he was telling this woman intimate details of his life that he couldn't even explain to Lena. Maybe it was the no-nonsense attitude she wrapped around herself like a shield. Or the soft center he sensed was hidden beneath. "She said no. It's over. I was the rebound guy, nothing more than an island fling."

"I'm not so sure about that."

But he was. Lena had no desire to take their affair further than this week. If she did, she would be leaving with him.

"Your call, Marcy. Do I pay for everything or contact my attorneys? And trust me, I have many who jump when I call."

With a growl, Marcy slapped the top of her desk. He heard Tina yelp out in the hallway and had no doubt Zane would be appearing again shortly. But one way or another, Colt would be gone before he appeared.

Reaching into his pocket, he pulled out his cell and began dialing.

"Fine. Stop. You win," she said.

Punching End, Colt slipped his cell back into his pocket. She didn't need to know that he'd been about to call himself. He wasn't going to bother his attorney this early, not when he already knew that he'd won.

"I'd like all digital and physical copies of the photographs, and I want them deleted from your computer so I know that they can't resurface anywhere."

Marcy narrowed her eyes but nodded.

"And if you could arrange for a private launch to pick me up at the dock, I'd appreciate it."

"The ferry will be here in a few hours."

"I didn't say ferry. I said private launch. And the sooner the better."

"It'll take at least an hour before they can get here."

"Fine, I'll wait. That should give you time to get any remaining pictures from Mikhail. And to erase the originals."

Marcy's mouth twisted in an unflattering frown. "I'll make a call."

Colt passed Zane in the hallway on his way out to the main lobby. The other man eyed Colt but didn't stop him. An hour later he was bumping across choppy seas, a bulging manila envelope tucked under his arm.

He couldn't keep himself from turning around and watching the line of the island as it receded into nothing.

LENA WANDERED ALONG the vacant beach, listening to the waves as they crashed against the sand. She'd walked along the shore many times since they'd arrived on the island.

Today it felt different. Instead of being warm and relaxing…it was lonely. Because she knew Colt wasn't lurking in the trees or waiting for her to return to their bungalow. He was gone.

Today was her last day on the island. Originally, they'd planned to take the later ferry, but Lena couldn't stand to sit here upset and alone.

She'd done the right thing. So why did it feel so bad?

Walking back to the bungalow, she threw the last few items into her suitcase and set it by the door so she'd be ready. She glanced quickly into the mirror above the sink, thinking how appropriate it was that she'd be leaving the island in much the same condition she'd come onto it—sleep deprived and miserable, with dark circles under her eyes.

The resort was beginning to bustle as sleepy guests stirred. It was late by most standards, but not for Escape. Here people indulged. How quickly she'd become used to the hedonistic pace.

She walked across the compound to the main building. Stopping at the front desk, she asked to speak with Marcy, hoping the other woman was already up and at work. The smiling clerk told her she'd be right out.

Unable to sit still, Lena walked across the empty lobby to the windows and the vista of sun, sand and waves outside. It looked beautiful. Too bad she was leaving the idyllic setting under less than happy circumstances.

"I thought I'd see you this morning," Marcy said as she walked up beside her.

"Oh?" Lena turned briefly to look at the other woman, working restlessly on the rings that still sat heavily on her finger. She spun them around and around.

"Colt came to see me yesterday."

Lena returned her gaze to the beautiful view out the window. Better than the pity she saw in Marcy's bright blue eyes.

"He's gone," Marcy said gently.

"I know. He got a call to take a job in Peru."

Marcy pulled a large manila envelope from behind her back. "These are for you. He demanded all of the copies, but I thought the least he owed you were the photographs."

Lena stared down at the nondescript brown paper and then back up at Marcy without actually touching it.

"What are you talking about?"

"He didn't tell you?"

"Tell me what?"

"Jeez, woman. Do the men in your life tell you anything? Colt bought the rights to all of the photographs."

Disbelief blasted through her and Lena turned to face Marcy fully.

"Why would he do that?"

Marcy shrugged. "You'll have to ask him, but I think it probably had something to do with keeping them private."

"That idiot," she breathed out.

"Oh, it gets better. He threatened to get his lawyers

involved and tie us up in the courts until the photographs were useless to me."

"It was a bluff."

"I don't think so."

Lena threw her hands up in the air. "What are you going to do? Don't you need the photos for your ad campaign?"

Marcy's frown was genuine, along with the lingering pique no doubt directed toward Colt. "Yep. Colt made some suggestions for an alternative." Her frown pulled into a reluctant smile. "And damn the man for being right."

"He's a great photographer," Lena admitted. While she might be upset, she couldn't deny his talent.

"He's paying for Mikhail to stay and shoot the new photographs."

"How much is this costing him?"

"You really don't want to know. Between the photos and the cost of your stay…"

"That's got to be thousands."

"Try about forty."

Anger bubbled up inside Lena. "I'm sorry. We both agreed to this and he shouldn't have reneged." A growl of frustration and unreleased sadness rolled through her. "I'd like to strangle him."

Marcy laughed. With a pointed look, she said, "You'll have to catch him first."

They both knew that wasn't going to happen. Lena turned back toward the window. The perfect setting was easier to deal with than anything Marcy was saying.

"Colt paid for an extra day, but I'm guessing it's a waste of breath to tell you to stay."

Lena nodded.

Marcy laid the envelope on the edge of a nearby table before saying, "The ferry should be here in about twenty minutes. I'll have someone fetch your luggage and meet you at the dock."

And like that, it was all over.

Again.

In the space of a week she'd lost two men. One she'd never loved but thought she had. And one she'd never considered loving until it was too late.

Marcy's words echoed through her head, *you'll have to catch him.* Part of her wanted to do just that. To chase after him like a love-starved puppy, eager for any crumbs he might throw. A restless need suffused her body, but she refused to give in to it.

She had her own life, her own identity, and she refused to give it up. This was the right decision for her.

A tiny voice in the back of her brain said *you thought that about Wyn once, too.* But she ignored it.

Slipping both rings off her finger, she shoved them deep into her pocket. Past and present hidden away. She probably should give the band back to Marcy, but she wouldn't…. Couldn't. Picking up the envelope, Lena tucked it under her arm and headed for the dock and the journey to the rest of her life.

Whatever that might hold.

14

She'd been home for a week. In that time, she'd managed to avoid her family and had formally quit her job. Mr. Rand had tried to get her to stay, and part of her had been tempted. Fear of the unknown almost made her accept his offer.

It felt wrong to be cut adrift with no real direction. She'd worked so hard to become successful. She'd even held two jobs to put herself through college.

For the first time since she'd turned sixteen, Lena had no responsibilities. No boss waiting for her to come in. No rush projects that would require all-nighters.

And she almost wished that she had. Being busy might have helped keep her mind off Colt. She wondered what he was doing and if he missed her. Probably not, he was out in the middle of the rain forest living his dream.

She slept late and unpacked. Once or twice she wandered the city like a tourist, seeing the sites she'd never made time to visit. Finding another job was high on her list of priorities, but she decided to put it off for a few weeks. Mr. Rand had offered her a generous severance package, which meant she had some breathing room.

Since the decision to push Colt out of her life had been hers, it seemed stupid to mope. But it was difficult not to. One day after quitting, Lena pulled out the bin of jewelry supplies she'd stuck deep in the back of her closet. Dust fluttered to the ground when she popped open the lid.

Semiprecious jewels, crystals, beads, gold wire and silver stared back at her like long-lost friends.

The first night she didn't stop until her stomach growled and her fingers were so sore she could barely continue the next morning. But she did anyway.

By the end of the fourth day she had an array of necklaces, earrings, bracelets and rings. Things she was proud of. She had no idea what to do with them, but she'd figure that out.

She'd figure out a way to make this a part of her life. Lena was through sacrificing pieces of herself. She enjoyed making jewelry and that was all that mattered. Even if she couldn't find a way to support herself with it, she wouldn't ever pack it away again.

A knock on the door startled her, causing her to drop a pair of small pliers, which clattered to the tabletop, scattering a handful of the peacock-blue beads she'd been working with.

Grumbling under her breath, Lena chased after them. She was ass up with her head as far under the couch as it could go when a deep voice sounded behind her. The back of her head cracked against the wooden edge of the couch frame. Adrenaline burst through her body. Holding her splitting head, she fell into a heap on the floor and managed to spin around at the same time.

Wyn was the last person she expected to find staring down at her sprawled body.

"What are you doing here? How the hell did you get in?"

Holding a shiny gold key in front of his face he said, "I came by to return this."

"And thought you'd use it one more time?"

"You didn't answer." His eyes shifted around the apartment, looking everywhere but at her. "I was worried about you."

He'd thought she'd be inconsolable. Or worse that she'd hurt herself. She could see it in his eyes, the sheepish realization that he'd jumped to the wrong conclusion. He probably would have preferred it if she had been comatose with despair.

"Don't flatter yourself, Wyn. I'm hardly a candidate for suicide watch because you slept with my cousin."

He shifted from one foot to the other and Lena realized he was nervous. Or maybe *uncomfortable* was a better word. Good.

Pushing up from the floor, Lena dropped the few beads she'd managed to find back onto the table. She and Wyn stared at each other, both at a loss for what to say next. More than the room and her scattered jewelry supplies stood between them. And probably always had.

"What's that?" Wyn asked, pushing his hands deep into his pockets and nodding toward the mess on the table.

"I've started designing jewelry again."

"That's good. I always thought you were great at it."

That was a revelation she hadn't expected. "Why didn't you ever say that?"

"You didn't seem to want my opinion on it. You were always so independent and capable. You never asked what I thought about your jewelry, or anything else for that matter."

"That's not true."

He shrugged.

"I definitely didn't ask you to sleep with my cousin."

A frown pulled the corners of his lips down and marred the perfect expanse of his brow. "I'm sorry about that, Lena. I honestly didn't mean for it to happen. I never meant to hurt you."

She blew a deep breath out of her lungs and sank slowly to the couch. She couldn't let him take all of the blame. Yes, he'd been the one to betray their relationship, but at that moment, Lena wondered if she'd given him any other option.

"You didn't, which probably says a lot." She waved her hands, dismissing his apology. "It doesn't matter. We didn't love each other, but neither one of us wanted to say so."

He might have taken the coward's way out, but then she almost had, too. She should have listened to the jitters—they'd been trying to tell her something, but she'd been unwilling to take a risk and let what was safe and comfortable go for the unknown.

"Doesn't excuse what I did."

"No, it doesn't."

"If it makes any difference, we're trying to make it work."

Shock had Lena staring at Wyn's face. Unable to help herself, she began to laugh. "God help you. You do realize that she's almost ten years younger than you are and one of the most helpless people I've ever met."

"That's okay. I like that she needs me. Besides, she makes me feel young."

"You *are* young, Wyn."

"Yeah, but sometimes I forget that. You've met my mother, can you blame me? I was a little adult before I started kindergarten, my entire life laid out for me like a Christmas suit."

Lena shook her head. "I suppose it makes sense in a weird way. She really is the opposite of everything you probably thought you wanted."

He laughed. "She's definitely the opposite of you."

"Don't I know it."

"I've been thinking about it a lot, and maybe that's why we didn't work. We're too much alike. Mitzi challenges me, infuriates me and makes me laugh. She sees things in a different way and makes me see them that way, too."

"You don't think that'll get old?"

"Who knows, but we're going to give it a try. We might end up hating each other or we might find that we're exactly what the other needs. I ground her to reality and she makes me pick my head up and look around every once in a while."

Unexpected jealousy spurted through Lena's veins. Not because Mitzi and Wyn had found happiness together. The fact that their relationship didn't bother her was just proof that she and Wyn had made the right decision in not getting married. But she envied that they'd found each other and had a camaraderie she hadn't felt since she'd walked off that island alone.

From the very beginning, she'd had that with Colt. A sense of easiness, a connection and kindred spirit. Oh, he knew exactly how to push her buttons, but he challenged her and prodded her and made her question her view of the world. Or he had until it had all fallen apart.

Even on the island, in their most intimate conversations, what had he done? Challenged her view. Most of the people who might have gone to that island with her would have plied her with alcohol and told her what a bastard Wyn was.

Not Colt. He'd held her own feet to the fire and made her look logically at the bigger picture. The man was insightful and brilliant in a way that she hadn't really given him credit for.

Silence stretched between Lena and Wyn, neither of them knowing what else there was to say.

"You don't have to quit. If anyone should leave the company it should be me."

"Please, we both know your dad would never let you do that."

"Actually, I think he'd rather have you than me."

Lena frowned. "I'm not coming back, and even if I was I wouldn't make you leave. You're good at your job, Wyn. Most of the time."

"Well, would you at least consider freelancing for

us? You're the best graphic designer we've got. You could work from home. Take the jobs that you wanted."

She stared at Wyn as if he'd suddenly grown another head. He was suggesting something that had never occurred to her, but that was definitely intriguing.

"I'll think about it." She had to consider all the angles before making a decision. What he was talking about was going into business for herself. That took planning and preparation. Rand Marketing couldn't be her only client if she intended to make a living.

But it was definitely a possibility. And she liked the idea of having more flexibility. Of being in complete control of her destiny.

A flash of guilt crossed Wyn's face. "So…uh…how was the honey—your trip?"

Lena lifted a single eyebrow and stared at him for several seconds. "Do you know what an idiot I looked like when Colt and I arrived at that resort?"

"Well, if things had gone according to plan you'd never have known the difference."

"Trust me, I would have noticed. Marcy makes drill sergeants look like fuzzy puppies. And Mikhail, the photographer, was good at blending in, but not that good."

"So you went through with it?" he asked, surprised.

"What choice did I have? I couldn't afford that place."

"I never liked Colt—I always thought there was more going on between you—" Lena tried not to look guilty "—but I figured he'd take care of everything for you."

"Oh, he did. After the photographs were already taken."

"Something tells me there's more to that story."

If only he knew. But she and Wyn had never had the same kind of relationship she'd once shared with Colt. They'd never talked in depth about their feelings. Never really shared their worries or struggles. Until that moment it was something she hadn't even been aware of.

"Maybe."

Wyn stepped closer, holding out his hand and offering the kind of comfort he'd never bothered with before. Lena didn't accept it. Somehow it would have felt wrong. Artificial.

"I know you well enough to realize that whatever happened, you aren't happy."

"Let's just say things got complicated."

"You mean you slept with him."

Lena resented the heat that flared up her face. It was pointless and all but screamed he was right. However, she refused to confirm his suspicions with words.

Wyn shook his head. "I know I'm probably the last person who should be doling out relationship advice, but I'm going to do it anyway. You and Colt are perfect for each other. It's one of the reasons I didn't like him. Whatever happened, it can't be bad enough to ruin the bond that you share."

"You're wrong. We're terrible for each other."

"*You're* wrong. He's adventurous and exotic. You're practical and grounded. You complement each other just like Mitzi balances me."

Lena frowned.

"Trying to make it work might be risky, but would the end result be worth it?" Wyn cocked his head to the side and studied her. For the first time since they'd met, she thought maybe he was really seeing her. "Do you love him?" he finally asked.

Lean nodded.

"Then go for it. Don't give up on love, Lena. I know from experience that it's a tricky thing to find. Don't let fear or duty or what everyone else expects hold you back. You have to take what you want."

This time when Wyn reached out to her, she let him wrap his arm around her shoulder. It felt weird, having him hold her. Now that she'd experienced the connection she shared with Colt, it was obvious there was nothing here. Nothing except for the kind offer of comfort.

"I've always thought of you as fearless. You don't take no for an answer. You set your sights on something and you work tirelessly until you get it. Why would love be any different? Decide what you want and fight for it. Until you win, or until there's no breath left in your body. Either way, you'll have no regrets."

She smiled up at him. "When did you get so smart?"

He laughed, bumping his shoulder against hers. "Almost two weeks ago, when an amazing woman walked away from me and I realized I'd almost screwed up several lives because I was a coward, too scared to break free from my family's expections."

"You've changed," she said. And definitely for the better. This Wyn, the one who was wise and insightful and understanding, was a far cry from the distant, charming man she'd been set to marry. Not that she was any more attracted to him. But this Wyn, she thought, might make a great friend.

"That's what happens when you get dropped into chaos and baptized by fire. You slipped off to a secluded island. I had to deal not only with my parents, but your mother, aunt and Mitzi, too."

Part of her wanted to grin. "I think I would have liked to see that."

"I assure you, it wasn't pretty. And I'm still paying for what I did, but that's okay."

"Oh, before I forget." Lena pulled out of Wyn's embrace and disappeared into her bedroom to retrieve the ring she'd placed in her jewelry box for safekeeping. The large diamond flashed as the light hit it, but it was the plain band sitting next to it that held her attention.

Walking back into the living room, she held the engagement ring out to Wyn. "Just promise me you won't rush into things and give it to Mitzi the minute you see her." She thought about her words, about everything Wyn had just said and the slow progression of their own relationship. "Wait. Scratch that. Maybe you *should* give it to her right away."

Wyn held out his hands, not to take what she offered, but to tell her to stop. "No, Lena, that's yours. Sell it. Keep it. I don't care. It's the least I owe you."

"You don't owe me anything, Wyn." Reaching for his hand, she turned it over, dropped the ring into his palm and curled his fingers around it. Giving him back the ring was the right thing to do. Not because it was expensive. Not because it mattered to either of them. But because it *didn't* matter and never really had. It was a symbol of the mistake they'd almost made, and keeping it around just felt wrong.

He looked up at her with a mixed expression of guilt and hope and something she hadn't seen in a long time but never realized was missing—happiness.

"I hope you can be happy, Lena."

Wyn left after she promised to give his father a call in a few days, once she'd thought about his offer to freelance. If nothing else, she might do it until she found a new job.

Wyn was gone, but his words still lingered in her head.

Was she being a coward? Was she allowing fear to rule her decisions and keep her from really living?

There was certainly no hiding the devastation she was feeling. No, she wasn't wallowing in her bed, but that didn't mean she wasn't heartbroken and upset.

She was definitely afraid. Afraid to put herself out there, to admit that she loved Colt, only to find out that he didn't feel the same. Or that they couldn't make their lives mesh. Or that he wanted something different from the future than she did.

How quickly he had dropped everything to rush off to Peru. It scared her, his ability to pull up stakes at a moment's notice. But a tiny part of her also envied him those adventures.

She had to admit that there were a few good things about her childhood, although she often had a hard time remembering them. She'd seen so many amazing things. She hadn't just taken history, she'd learned about all the ancient sites in person. There were memories, good ones, of sharing laughter and happy times with her mother. It was just that they'd been overshadowed by the helplessness, fear and uncertainty of the bad times.

But could she continue to let those bad memories and unwanted lessons dictate her future?

How did she know for sure that she and Colt couldn't make it work? She hadn't given them the chance to try.

Hell, if Wyn and Mitzi could make it work, anyone could.

That left only one thing for her to do.

Go to Peru.

COLT LET HIS EYES WANDER the dark jungle surrounding the camp. Off to the right, several of the team huddled around a campfire joking, laughing and drinking bad coffee. Normally, he'd have been right there with them enjoying the rugged parts of the job that forced him to rely on his own skills and instincts.

Not tonight. Actually, not since he'd gotten there. All he'd thought about was Lena.

How she'd turned him down. How he'd walked away.

He'd thought long and hard about what had been different between them on the island. Was it that she'd been free? Was it the romantic, sensual atmosphere of the place?

Colt didn't think so.

"I'm an idiot," he said to no one in particular.

High up in a tree, a monkey chattered back at him.

Colt strained to make out the features of the animal in the dark, but could only see the barest outline. The leaves rustled as the monkey crept closer. It was almost eerie, the way the animal stared at him, as if it expected an explanation.

For some reason, Colt responded. "I was scared. Everyone gets scared," he defended, as if the monkey could understand. He, the guy who fearlessly jumped into any new adventure, had been scared of practical, grounded Lena. Scared to take a risk and find out that she didn't love him the way he loved her. Scared to have her and lose her.

Although that had happened anyway.

And now it was worse, because he didn't even have their friendship anymore.

The night he'd gotten the call that his parents' helicopter had gone down in a forest in North Carolina, he'd been devastated. Until then, the only person he'd ever lost was his grandmother and it hadn't been a shock. But that phone call...it had floored him. He hadn't known what to do. What to think. Where to turn.

But Lena had been there. She was the first person he'd called, and she'd rushed over. He'd relied so heavily on her for emotional and moral support. And that had scared him even more. Somewhere in the haze of grief and anger that had followed, he'd convinced himself that it was better to be alone than to risk feeling the pain of losing someone he loved again.

It was easy to push everyone in his life away. Lena, his brother, sister-in-law and niece, none of them could come with him as he directed his career to far off places. Yes, part of him relished the adventure that fueled some innate need. But he could have found that elsewhere. He could have gone to L.A. or New York and found work in a more traditional setting.

But working on documentaries allowed him to slip away into the world and get lost in his art.

And he'd thought he was happy and satisfied—until Lena's life exploded in front of him. He'd been there for her—there was no question that he would be. He'd have walked to the ends of the earth if she needed him.

That kiss. That stupid, wonderful, innocent kiss had changed everything. From that moment on, his curiosity about what being with Lena might be like had become impossible to ignore. There was no more pretending or trying to shunt his desire and awareness of her away.

He loved her, had always loved her, even if he hadn't been able to admit it to himself. He'd been scared of loving her only to lose her. But he'd lost her anyway because he was an idiot and hadn't told her the truth, the reason he wanted her with him.

When he'd asked her to go to Peru, he hadn't told her the thought of living without her made him crazy. And when she'd said no, what had he done?

Used his work once more to escape from the pain. The only problem was that it had followed him, sharper than ever now that she wasn't there.

He should have told her he loved her.

The monkey began to rattle the branch that it perched on, as if upset it was being ignored. "What am I doing here?" Colt asked it. The little creature, its white face materializing out of the darkness as it leaned down, cocked its head to the side and stared at Colt as if it'd finally figured out the million-dollar question… and was still waiting for him to clue in to the answer.

He shouldn't be here. He should be with Lena. The realization was crystal clear. The monkey opened its mouth, chattering some syllables only it understood. Colt almost reached toward it but at the last minute noticed the gleaming sharp teeth in its open mouth. Instead, he backed away slowly.

Raking his gear up into a pile as quickly as possible, he began assembling what he'd need to get back out to the nearest village.

"What are you doing?" one of the camera crew asked, breaking away from the pack of people.

"I have to go home."

"Now? Colt, we're just getting started. We need you here. Desmond is not going to like this."

Colt glanced up at the group of people who'd stopped talking and were now all staring at him, a tight circle that looked almost as dangerous as the monkey he'd left behind.

"We're doing fine. I'll be back in a few days. A week at the most. You know the schedule. Continue to shoot the footage that we talked about and I'll go over it when I get back."

Thirty minutes after talking to the monkey, Colt was headed out of the Peruvian jungle and home to Lena. He had no idea what was going to happen…but it was about damn time that he found out.

15

WYN WAS RIGHT. When Lena chose to go after something, she did it with a vengeance.

Twenty-four hours following her decision to go, she was winging her way to Peru. As it turned out, she'd needed to get up to date on her vaccinations. Her doctor had even given her a rabies shot, since she thought Lena would probably end up in remote locations.

And she was right. It had taken her several hours to get in touch with Desmond. The man was difficult to track down. But he'd been happy to tell her what village Colt's team had traveled out of when she'd explained the situation.

Unfortunately, she'd arrived too late in the day and had been forced to rent a room for the night. None of the villagers she'd spoken to had been willing to make the trek into the jungle so close to dark.

Lena was frustrated. She'd come all this way only to be stopped by someone else's fear, but she couldn't really blame them. She knew firsthand that the jungle was a dangerous place after dark.

Her room left something to be desired. It was clean, although in serious need of a facelift. However, the woman who ran the place had bent over backwards to make sure she felt at home. Probably because Lena was currently the only guest.

Although she had to admit that there was something nice about sitting in a cane rocker on the screened-in front porch. The tiny village bustled with activity as the residents ended their work for the day and disappeared into their own houses. As she watched, the open-air market closed up for the night. The colorful awnings that had protected the wares were rolled up and stored for morning.

The heat might have been unbearable except for the lazy rotation of a fan high above her. The thick manila envelope lay in her lap. Packing for the trip, she'd found the photographs she'd left unopened in the bottom of her suitcase. She hadn't stopped to look at them until she got on the plane.

Her hand rested softly over the envelope, warming the paper beneath her palm. She'd been...surprised by what she'd seen. If she'd needed any more proof that she was making the right decision, it had been captured in the photographs Colt had worked so hard to keep private.

She could understand his insistence now, and appreciated his forethought. They were intimate, personal, and she had no desire to share them with the world.

Stars began to appear in the sky above her, brighter than anything she'd ever seen.

Far down the main path, a figure appeared, materializing out of the lush green brush that bordered the village. For some reason she watched, drawn to the man long before she could clearly see him.

It was obvious he wasn't local. He was taller than most of the native people she'd met and walked with a purposeful stride that seemed foreign here.

He was halfway past when she bolted up out of her chair.

"Colt," she breathed.

The screen door slapped, springing backward as she rushed through it.

Again she said his name, only this time yelling it. "Colt!"

He stopped, the sudden shuffle of his feet kicking up a cloud of dust around his ankles. He stared at her as she ran toward him, his eyes wide with surprise.

"Lena," he said, "what are you doing here?"

She wanted to launch herself into his arms. The sheer joy of seeing him was so overwhelming that she could hardly contain it. But she wasn't certain of her reception, so she didn't. Instead, she halted several paces away.

He looked good, although she had no idea what she'd expected. He'd only been gone a week.

"I came to find you."

"Find me?" he asked, parroting her words. "But I was heading back home to you."

She laughed, elation filling the sound. That was a good sign, right? All the fear and anxiety that had been riding her for the past twenty-four hours dried away to nothing.

A couple of times she'd almost chickened out, convinced that it was madness to follow him to Peru. But she'd clamped down on the doubts and told herself to get over it. It was difficult to ignore years of conditioned reactions and emotions, but for Colt she was willing to try.

Rolling up her sleeve, she showed him the tiny round bandages that covered her vaccination spots. "I even got shots."

Colt reached down and grabbed her, lifting her up off the ground and crushing her against his body. He stared down into her face. The sheer intensity in his gaze overwhelmed her, but not nearly as much as the love she could now see clearly in the depths of his eyes. Had it always been there and she'd just been afraid to accept it? Or, like her, had their days apart been enough to make him realize what they had together?

"Do you need me to kiss them and make them better?" he finally rumbled.

A welcome shiver of awareness racked her body. She wanted him to kiss her senseless, but there was plenty of time to give in to the passion pumping deep and dark inside her. They had more important things to deal with first.

"Maybe later. Why were you going home?"

"Why are you in Peru?"

She pursed her lips, wiggling in his hold and silently asking to be released. He ignored her.

"I've always wanted to see Machu Picchu," she answered.

"Huh," he grunted, obviously not convinced by her lie. "Too bad it's not anywhere close."

"Why were you leaving? I thought you had a job to do. The break you've been waiting years for."

"I do. But none of that mattered without you," he whispered.

A sense of peace stole through her body. They'd find a way to make it work.

"Good thing I've cleared my calendar, then. That way you can have your cake and me, too."

"What about your life in D.C.? Your job, apartment, friends?"

"I don't have a job."

"He fired you? What an idiot."

Lena chuckled, appreciating the heat of Colt's support. "Actually, he didn't. I quit and he offered me a severance package. And then a position freelancing for the company."

"Freelancing?"

"I'm seriously considering it. Once I've built my client base I could work from just about anywhere. Even from the middle of the Peruvian jungle."

Colt stared down at her, speechless. Finally, he licked his tongue across his lips and cautiously asked, "What, exactly, does that mean?"

"It means that I can follow you wherever you go… whether you want me there or not."

"I want you there." His mouth claimed hers in a hot, hard kiss that didn't last nearly long enough. "Always. Anywhere. I want you with me, Lena. But I'd happily settle for a little house in the suburbs of D.C. I'd settle for anywhere you wanted to be."

"Good thing for you where I want to be is with you. For now, we can gallivant around the world. Later, when we have kids, I'll want to talk about settling down and giving them some roots, but there are always summers and school breaks."

She smiled up into Colt's bright eyes and realized something that should have been clear years ago.

"All these years, I've been searching for roots. For a sense of the stability I never had as a child. Until you left, I didn't realize that having roots means surrounding yourself with people you love, trust and respect. It's about having a partner to share your life with—good and bad. It has nothing to do with one specific place."

"Well, hell, I could have told you that."

"So what made you change your mind?" she asked, snuggling tighter against his chest.

"I realized I love you. And have for years. I was too scared to admit it, to risk what we already had and open myself to the potential for more pain. It was easier to pretend that I was happy alone. I was so afraid to lose you, but by not admitting how I felt I lost you anyway."

He pulled back, making sure that she saw him when he said, "I love you, Lena, and I need you in my life."

"Well, for better or worse, you've got me."

A few minutes earlier, Lena would have claimed there was nothing Colt could say that would surprise her. She'd have been wrong.

"Does that mean you'll marry me?" he asked, his lips brushing down the side of her neck.

Lena didn't know what to say. Her heart fluttered inside her chest. Until that moment she hadn't realized that's what she'd wanted to hear. But even as she wanted to scream yes, a bone-deep need for caution welled up inside her. Old habits were hard to break.

"Maybe it's a little too soon? I mean, two weeks ago I was marrying someone else."

A wicked gleam drifted into Colt's eyes and Lena suddenly had the urge to turn tail and run. "What difference does that make? You have a dress—a beautiful dress that looked amazing on you, by the way. Bridesmaids. The groomsmen would have to change, but I bet we could have this wedding ready in no time flat. I want to make this legal, bind you to me so you can't leave."

"I'm not going anywhere."

His arms tightened around her, arching her body into his so that she couldn't help but feel the hard press of his erection lodged between them. "You better not be."

"Don't you have a film to direct or something?" she asked breathlessly.

"Yes, but that won't take forever," he answered as he bent down to taste the hollow of her throat. His hot mouth seared her skin. Her fingers dug deeper into his shoulders. "Besides, if we get married right away you can come back here with me as my wife."

Lena's head was spinning, a combination of lust for the man holding her and the feeling that she was getting everything she ever wanted…just a little faster than she'd planned.

"We both know that I can get you to say yes, Lena."

His hand skimmed down over her body. Need blasted through her, hot and hard.

"That's playing dirty."

"Maybe." His mouth sucked at the racing pulse at the base of her throat. "But I'll take what I can get."

She was on fire. And happy. And for the life of her, she couldn't come up with a reason not to say yes. She'd been ready to tie her life to a man who was completely wrong for her just two weeks ago. Then, she'd had jitters that she ignored. Now, the only thing jangling inside was an insistent little voice that said if they didn't find a bed soon the entire village was going to be shocked.

"Bring it on," she said, laughing with happiness when he spun her around.

They *were* perfect for each other. They had a history and a friendship that was the solid base for so much more.

She'd gone to the island hoping to find a few days of peace. To figure out how to put the pieces of her life back together. Instead, she'd found the love of her life…a man who'd been standing in front of her the whole time. She'd scoffed about the legend of Île du Coeur, but maybe there was more to it she thought.

And when they were old and gray, they'd show their grandchildren the pictures from the island where they found their hearts' desire.

Epilogue

MARCY WATCHED AS Lena and Colt boarded the ferry back to St. Lucia. They'd only stayed for a few days to celebrate their honeymoon—something about finishing a project in Peru. But they'd promised to return often, and despite all the trouble they'd caused her, Marcy was looking forward to having them back. She liked those two. And she liked the fact that they'd both woken up and realized they were meant to be.

"Don't tell me you have a romantic side after all. It'll ruin my opinion of you."

Marcy's back stiffened at the sound of Simon's voice behind her. For once, she wished her boss had stayed locked inside his office where she'd left him.

"I have no such thing. Romance is a big hoax, lust wrapped up in a pretty package so that everyone feels better about their animalistic tendencies."

Simon walked up beside her, folding his arms over his chest and staring out after the ferry as it pulled into the bright blue water.

"You know, if you'd take that stick out of your ass,

Marcy, you might actually find that life is usually enjoyable. Oh, and that sex isn't half bad."

"You know nothing about my sex life, Simon, so stop pretending that you do."

He shrugged, his careless attitude pissing her off even more than his little digs. Part of her wanted him to care, wanted him to wonder who and what she was. But that was just asking for trouble.

And she had enough of that where Simon was concerned.

"The photography team will be here at the end of the week. I've cleared the new concept with *Worldwide Travel*. Everyone seems excited and I'm hopeful it might actually work out better."

"That's good, considering you're the one who screwed it up in the first place."

Marcy ground her teeth to keep from saying something that would get her fired. *I need this job, I need this job,* she chanted silently.

Simon hadn't even cared about the first photo shoot. And, honestly, she'd eat her own shoe if he cared about this one. He just loved the fact that he could throw the hiccup in her face.

Without waiting for her response—*coward*—Simon turned around and strode off. He was halfway up the walk when she remembered that she'd needed to talk to him about the shoot. She hated how he could make her forget things. It drove her insane.

"Simon," she called.

He turned to look at her, and she could tell by the faraway, distracted expression in his blue eyes that he'd already gone somewhere else. She wondered where it was, this place that could so easily engross him. Normally it bugged the hell out of her, especially when she wanted his attention. But today it worked in her favor, since he wasn't going to like what she needed to ask.

"The production crew would like to shoot in your office. It's the highest floor in the main building and the backdrop of the water and sky should work perfectly for the concept we're using."

She watched as he shook his head, trying to focus on what she was saying. That might not be good.

Before he could come around, she added, "I just wanted to remind you that you'd agreed to let them shoot there." Waving her hands, she sighed in relief as Simon turned on his heel and walked away.

She might regret that later—as in when the crew showed up at his office door—but she'd worry about it then.

She'd gotten awfully good at putting off until tomorrow what she didn't have to worry about today.

Her sigh of relief was a bit premature—at the head of the path Simon paused and turned slowly back toward her, pinning her with his eyes. Gone was the preoccupied expression, replaced by a sharp glint that had unwanted heat suffusing her body.

Marcy yanked her gaze away, swallowing. She did not want Simon Reeves.

Hell, she didn't even like the man....

* * * * *

PASSION

For a spicier, decidedly hotter read—
this is your destination for romance!

COMING NEXT MONTH
AVAILABLE FEBRUARY 28, 2012

#669 TIME OUT
Jill Shalvis

#670 ONCE A HERO...
Uniformly Hot!
Jillian Burns

#671 HAVE ME
It's Trading Men!
Jo Leigh

#672 TAKE IT DOWN
Island Nights
Kira Sinclair

#673 BLAME IT ON THE BACHELOR
All the Groom's Men
Karen Kendall

#674 THE PLAYER'S CLUB: FINN
The Player's Club
Cathy Yardley

REQUEST YOUR FREE BOOKS!
2 FREE NOVELS PLUS 2 FREE GIFTS!

red-hot reads!

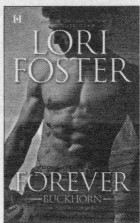

New York Times *and* USA TODAY *bestselling author*
Maya Banks presents book three in her miniseries
PREGNANCY & PASSION.

TEMPTED BY HER INNOCENT KISS

Available March 2012 from Harlequin Desire!

There came a time in a man's life when he knew he was well and truly caught. Devon Carter stared down at the diamond ring nestled in velvet and acknowledged that this was one such time. He snapped the lid closed and shoved the box into the breast pocket of his suit.

He had two choices. He could marry Ashley Copeland and fulfill his goal of merging his company with Copeland Hotels, thus creating the largest, most exclusive line of resorts in the world, or he could refuse and lose it all.

Put in that light, there wasn't much he could do except pop the question.

The doorman to his Manhattan high-rise apartment hurried to open the door as Devon strode toward the street. He took a deep breath before ducking into his car, and the driver pulled into traffic.

Tonight was the night. All of his careful wooing, the countless dinners, kisses that started brief and casual and became more breathless—all a lead-up to tonight. Tonight his seduction of Ashley Copeland would be complete, and then he'd ask her to marry him.

He shook his head as the absurdity of the situation hit him for the hundredth time. Personally, he thought William Copeland was crazy for forcing his daughter down Devon's throat.

Ashley was a sweet enough girl, but Devon had no desire

to marry anyone.

William had other plans. He'd told Devon that Ashley had no head for the family business. She was too softhearted, too naive. So he'd made Ashley part of the deal. The catch? Ashley wasn't to know of it. Which meant Devon was stuck playing stupid games.

Ashley was supposed to think this was a grand love match. She was a starry-eyed woman who preferred her animal-rescue foundation over board meetings, charts and financials for Copeland Hotels.

If she ever found out the truth, she wouldn't take it well.

And hell, he couldn't blame her.

But no matter the reason for his proposal, before the night was over, she'd have no doubts that she belonged to him.

What will happen when Devon marries Ashley?
Find out in Maya Banks's passionate new novel
TEMPTED BY HER INNOCENT KISS
Available March 2012 from Harlequin Desire!

USA TODAY bestselling author

Carol Marinelli

begins a daring duet.

THE SECRETS *of* XANOS

Two brothers alike in charisma and power;
separated at birth and seeking revenge…

Nico has always felt like an outsider. He's turned his back on his
parents' fortune to become one of Xanos's most powerful exports
and nothing will stand in his way—until he stumbles
upon a virgin bride….

Zander took his chances on the streets rather than spending another
moment under his cruel father's roof. Now he is unrivaled in
business—and the bedroom! He wants the best people around him,
and Charlotte is the best PA! Can he tempt her
over to the dark side…?

A SHAMEFUL CONSEQUENCE
Available in March

AN INDECENT PROPOSITION
Available in April